2020 International Cultural Exchange Conference and 2020 International Environment Protection Awareness Conference

Editors of Proceedings:

David Zhang and Serena Mao

Ordering Information:

For orders and inquiries, please contact:
1-888-404-1388
www.goldtouchpress.com
book.orders@goldtouchpress.com

Printed in the United States of America

Table of Contents

Acknowledgments

We would like to thank all of our guest speakers for attending our conferences and providing us with such insightful speeches. We also thank our hosts for keeping the conference running smoothly, as well as the technology department for making sure the PowerPoint was working properly. Thank you to all the students who translated on stage, as well as those who transcribed and translated speeches for our proceedings.

Editors of Proceedings:
David Zhang and Serena Mao

English to Chinese Translators and Interpreters:
Brian Wu, Eileen Guo, Kevin Zhang, David Zhang

Proceedings Transcription:
David Zhang, Serena Mao, Ariel Yang, Cindy Wang, Ryan Li, Kevin Zhang, Owen Xu, Alice Zhong

Technical Support:
Zeru Peter Li

Hosts:
Serena Mao, David Zhang, Alice Zhong, Eileen Guo, Cindy Wang, Brian Wu, Kevin You, Kevin Zhang, Allen Bryan, Ariel Yang, Ryane Li

Host in China:
Zhuotong Xian

2020 International Cultural Exchange Conference

Location: online; Date: August 1, 2020

This has been the sixth annual International Cultural Exchange Conference. Our purpose for this conference is to have professionals and students exchange information and ideas about the differences between cultures ranging from the United States to China to Mexico, as well as providing insight into education abroad. We have translated, transcribed, compiled, and edited the speeches of all our speakers.

Proceeding editors: David Zhang

Eric Williams

I am Eric Williams. In 1997, I founded The Silver Room in the heart of Hyde Park, Chicago, as a way to support local designers, host events, and build community. It not only showcases art and culture but also provides a way for people to make some money in our neighborhood. This is what I have been focused on. Today I will talk about something slightly different though. I will get to what I do. But I think it is important that I first lay the groundwork for what I do from a historical context.

African Americans' Contribution to the Arts During Uncertain Times

The last few months have been very difficult for everybody around the world, especially for a lot of folks in America. We have had the pandemic and the civil unrest in response to police activity, the murder of a citizen named George Floyd. Those two incidents- the pandemic and the civil unrest have caused a lot of tension in our country.

A lot of my friends are artists. We have a lot of time on our hands because of the pandemic and the civil unrest. It's really interesting to see how an artist will respond to everything that's going on either visually or musically. I want to set a little groundwork of how this plays a part. Historically we've always done this. African Americans have always contributed to arts and culture during these times of unrest.

SINGING & DANCING ON PLANTATION CIRCA 1800s

This is a photo of what would have been slaves on their day off. Historically per the tradition of their culture, they had Sunday day off. So there would be singing, dancing, and storytelling, which was one day of celebration that American Africans would have during the time of slavery.

CONGO SQUARE

This picture is from New Orleans where Jazz was created in a place called Congo square. A lot of their music historically came from Africa. In New Orleans, it was a mixture of French Creole music and African rhythms, which became jazz.

During this time in the early nineteen hundreds as America was growing, many black Americans moved from the south to the north. It was called The Great Migration. It was the largest migration of people in human history. So they went from the south to many northern cities like Chicago, Detroit, and New York City.

HARLEM RENAISSANCE

During this time many black Americans took factory or service jobs because many black Americans weren't allowed to have certain higher-paying jobs. They were forced to do more menial labor.

Because of this, a cultural revolution was born. One of the main places that this happened was New York City, Harlem in New York City. Because of the hard life, they were living, they wanted to celebrate and be even more creative. As a response to racism in their heart, music was the way to celebrate. In Harlem, we had something called the big bands. Big huge jazz music bands, dancers, writers, and poets were all part of this movement called the Harlem Renaissance.

BRONZEVILLE, CHICAGO

This is a very famous photo from Chicago in the neighborhood where I live. It shows how a lot of black folks looked and dressed in the 1930s and 1940s. This is a place of culture and a place of music. Many famous people came out of Chicago during that time, mostly focusing on jazz music and blues music.

During this time, people were very creative. We still faced a lot of racism and opposition to what we're trying to do in the US. When soldiers came back post World War II, they had difficult times integrating into society because of racism. They could not find proper housing and jobs. It was a very very difficult time, but still, people were very creative.

BIRTH OF ROCK N' ROLL

As we moved further, the music evolved. This was music created by African-Americans called rock n' roll, which had its origin in jazz and blues. Rock n' roll music in its beginning was a response to the political environment in the US. Many of the performers and artists were unable to even show their faces on album covers because people in this country didn't want to see black faces.

MOTOWN

As we moved to the 1950s, 1960s, and early 70s, a movement of music called Motown was born in Detroit. A lot of the music was very new. It often had four or five people singing, dressed very nicely. This was again a response to a time of civil unrest in many ways. During the 1960s, there were a lot of marchings inspired by Martin Luther King protesting for civil rights. At the same time, Motown was born which was just beautiful music.

SOUL TRAIN

Another war ended in the early 1970s. You had this moment of freedom. You see the big afros?? that was a political statement for many people, a sense of freedom and dancing. This was a TV show called Soul Train. It was very important for African-Americans to see black people on TV celebrating, singing, and dancing for the first time. It is also a political movement through music and art.

DISCO

In the late 70s, disco music represented the cultural movement through music and dance. It created a sense of togetherness. In night clubs throughout America, people were able to celebrate in large masses of music and movement. In some ways, the start of dance music around the world was born out of these night clubs in New York City and Chicago.

The 1970s was a very hard time economically for everyone but especially black people. This was again a response to the harsh economic times that were happening in our country.

HIP HOP

As we moved into the early 80s, hip hop music was born. This was again started in New York City as a response to so many problems and issues that were happening in our major cities across America. In the 70s and early '80s, people felt they didn't have a place as part of society due to a lack of jobs and resources. So we created our places. Hip hop was born out of that through dancing and rapping. It was a way to tell our stories to each other.

BEYONCÉ

Now you see it happening in our modern-day. Artist Beyonce is basing a lot of her singing and her performance on history that happened. The music now is protest music. So it is not only entertainment but also is giving voice to a generation of people who maybe don't feel like they have a voice. This is where we are right now. Beyonce is a good example of an artist's response in a time of uncertainty.

THE SILVER ROOM

This is a photo of The Silver Room that I founded. This has been a place for many African Americans in Chicago to host events, to perform, to sing, to have art shows, and to read poetry. Because we have given a platform to these artists to showcase all forms of art, it has become a very important cultural staple in Chicago despite its limited space.

THE SILVER ROOM BLOCK PARTY

This is an event that I do every year. It is called The Silver Room Block Party. Last year, over 50,000 people came. I was showing you those pictures earlier to give you an idea of what legacy means to me, what history means to me, and how you can be informed from your history. All the music from before, the cultural events,... I think about those things in modern days. This event for me is a celebration of our culture. It's music. It is dancing. It is bringing people together in a very peaceful way. Sometimes especially for black Americans, we are seen in a way that is not always fair. So for me, we must have something that is a positive event, that not only we can see but the world can see the positivity of arts and culture.

Even though all of us are going through very difficult times now, I am hopeful that some form of new art will come from this time in America. The economy is up and down. We're trying to figure out what's next. However, I feel hopeful that, especially as African Americans, it is a time for us to be creative and to respond in a very positive way. I look forward to what the future will hold for us.

Dr. Jay Jones

Professor Jones has a broad academic background, with concentrations in Botany, Microbiology, Chemistry, and Geology. His research and work experience includes Senior Research Geobotanist, researching oil and gas exploration (ARCO), Naturalist/Interpreter (National Park Service), Remote Sensing Consultant (NASA/Lockheed). He is currently in the field conducting floral surveys, as well as in the laboratory working with complex analytical instrumentation. As Professor of Biology and Biochemistry, Jones has taught an exceptionally broad range of courses including versions of an interdisciplinary course entitled: Toward a Sustainable Planet. Many of these courses have field components in which faculty and students see the global impact of the human species in various countries around the world.

The American Higher Education

I'm going to be talking about higher education and specifically what you should get out of it. Most people seek higher education to qualify for specific jobs; I want to be in position, I want to be a lawyer, an engineer, etc. Another reason why people seek higher education is simply to make more money they see this as a way to gain wealth and then we also have to recognize that when you have a degree there is a certain level of prestige that goes along with that so those are the three different reasons that most people will actually go to a university or college but higher education should really open doors and allow you to see many paths that you may not have had before you actually entered about 70 percent of students change their major before they graduate and that is that is a that is not a bad statistic it's actually a good statistic because it means that students have found a pathway that they were not aware of before that that is more in line with their true desires personally I loved biology and chemistry and when I entered college I thought that pharmacy was the only path that I could take that would allow me to enjoy both biology and chemistry when I actually got into college it took me less than one term to realize I did not want to be a pharmacist I learned more about what pharmacy involved and I saw lots of other pathways to take so what I realized is that I had a lot of benefits that I did not expect so my education was already starting to be more than I had anticipated I had a passion for research better understanding of the major areas of human knowledge and how they fit together a deeper understanding of my own culture and traditions and an appreciation of the culture and traditions of others this is probably one of the most important things is to be in an environment where you learn about other cultures and when you understand that your own little cocoon is not necessarily a very good representation of reality so in essence it provided a better understanding of myself and my relationship to the universe so for me college opened up the doors and the windows so that I could see much more than I had been able to see without having that that expanding experience. The power to stretch your awareness to see the bigger picture the power to understand and appreciate other cultures the ability to assess information critically and get closer to the truth and the importance of values when making decisions in life, the ability to lead a more fulfilling life now these last two things are really really important because we're all citizens of a global war of a global environment and we need to make decisions in life that are consistent with understanding the impact of those decisions that we make and then finally we are at the brink of a system that is destined to collapse because of the current paradigm that we have to have infinite growth and we cannot have infinite growth in a finite environment so we need to concentrate on the ability to lead a more fulfilling life that is one of the elements that I believe very firmly needs to be part of higher education curriculum well don't tell us foreign so as as mr delgado has already indicated that a lot of the education at a college or university is outside of the classrooms it's in the dormitories dining halls public spaces etc and we're exposed to the thoughts and values of others when it if we remain in our own neighborhood we're not exposed to those thoughts I might share with reference to Mr. William's talk that I grew up in springfield illinois and that's the land of lincoln and this of course would have an image of being an area that really stresses equity racial equity and so forth and that town when I was young was very segregated it wasn't overt racism but racism nevertheless when I went to southern illinois university which is in carbondale a large number of Chicago students black chicago students were there and I became more aware of the of the black culture and it I might also add it was a time of great social upheaval and social engagement by the college students and other youthand then finally here many colleges are located in areas where students can actually reconnect with nature. We live in an isolated world and I feel it's important to be able to reconnect. So extracurricular learning takes place in many different places associated with the universities being able to keep in touch with nature. The upper right-hand image is from the top of a mountain that is very close to the university that I teach in. In the upper left-hand corner, you have an image of Walden pond, a very famous pond that is very near Harvard and MIT. So there are many different places that you can go to be reconnected with nature but I think that's an important thing to consider if you're trying to choose a university or college general education I can't stress this more both of both Mr. Schmidt and Delgado talked about Roosevelt's statement that if you're going to have a successful democracy you've got to have a strong educational system and that requires that you have general education courses so they're not necessarily going to be the courses that will make you a dentist or a geographer or a psychologist they are courses that broaden you that give you the big picture so that you can chart a course that's more consistent with your own goals and with the goals of and in my view college or university education should help you develop values that are consistent with the common good, not just thinking about your success. Also, travel can be an important component of Education to get out of one's own country and one's own culture is extremely important those students that I've taken a break off and come back and they say that it changed because in America here we have our review of what the world is all about and we do not have that sense of reality and that's true. I think in most countries if you can get out of your own country you get to see things much more broadly, you get to see the positive and the negative of the country that you're visiting as well as your own country. Travel can be important.

Traveling to Costa Rica with students informed me that my coffee addiction results in the conversion of acreage of tropical rainforests to coffee plantations which displaces natural vegetation and animals so it expanded my awareness. Okay let's see is that the next one might ask themselves if you're thinking of going and course there many different places in the world where you touching outside of the United States we have many different types of educational institutions some of them are State some of them are private and some of them are for-profit and so there are many different options that you can have and it doesn't matter what school you have there's a certain amount of marketing that is involved in promoting those institutions.

So in essence you need to care about what you want from your college education if you want to become a dentist or physician or engineer that you want to look for a school that has strong programs in those areas do you want Prestige is that your primary goal then you're going to want to go to one of the more prestigious School Stanford or Harvard and Princeton is it your goal to make connections for life because some of these institutions will give you connections to people who are in power and that can also enable you to move ahead more efficient are there other reasons that you can go to universities of one reason to go to university would be to answer the big questions in life just to learn more about the universe around us and then there are some students that just want to get away from home party okay for going to so you got to think about where you want to go Phyllis talk about where are you today. SLI go community colleges 2-year colleges they don't offer a bachelor's degrees but they're good Avenue to get you to a 4-year College they're extremely inexpensive self-motivated is the traditional 4-year universities and these can be either the state or private undergraduate universities with master's program so they have some graduate offering no doctor and then you have the finances. In the United States, we rank C's research.

So what is the best college for me to get what I'm looking for? How well-prepared are you into an institution that you're not prepared to succeed in? How much individual attention will I need in the physical and cultural environment? How much will it cost? That can be important all right. State versus private colleges each has their advantages you're going to probably pay a lot more if you go to private colleges but by and large they're going to provide you with a similar education comprehensive doctoral granting Institutions the R1 highly research centered institutions I do not recommend that students go to these for an undergraduate education in most cases they are concentrating on the research and and you're probably not going to get the attention that you would at let's say a second rank state school or private Institution it's and there are some factors here that are related to that okay i've covered that now I want to provide one caution and and that is that beware of the for-profit institutions some of them provide adequate training and so forth but there are a lot of for-profit institutions that are simply there to make money and and you don't want to be putting a lot of money out to and not get a good education there is an overall trend for the commodification of education and that is even occurring in my university where requirements are being reduced and curriculum simplified and so forth to simply attract more students now we can look specifically at the at the sars cove 2 effects and in our institution it is accelerating this commodification for a long time they've wanted us to go more toward virtual labs and so forth that require less instrumentation and supplies and I'm afraid that that the total online that we had for the better part of the last semester and probably much of this semester is going to accelerate that well you did it you went online before and you didn't have these expenses well I think you can do it continuously so I don't know what's going to come out of this but I travel is limited so we can't take our students anywhere we'll see what comes out of it but I really worry about the effects we do have administrative bloat more administrators and fewer faculty risk management is coming into this and I think i'll skip over this material because I understand that this will be available for people to look at after the program is over so you can kind of sort through this and any questions and so forth I'll be glad to answer but the education I let me just close by saying that the education I received is the most valuable thing in my life even if I never got a job. I would value the increased perspective that I have and the fact that I believe I'm a better global citizen for that education. Thank you for your attention.

Mr. Carl Scmidt

Carl Schmidt is a Business Education teacher at Monta Vista High School in Cupertino, California. He is one of the founders of Silicon Valley DECA, one of three California Districts. He just ended his second term as Chairperson of the California Association of DECA.

Mr. Schmidt completed his undergraduate work in Economics and later earned both a Masters Of Business Administration (International Business) and a Master of Arts in Education (Educational Leadership). Before his teaching career, he was a senior consultant for Price Waterhouse in New York City and both a Manager, Information Systems, and Materials Manager for Xerox Corporation's Southern California Manufacturing Operations. He also had the opportunity to serve as a co-founder and Executive Vice President of a Global Electronics start-up.

Key Values of American Culture

Good evening, and first of all, I want to thank Eric for a wonderful presentation. I think Eric is demonstrating something that's very, very important.

America is made up of many different stories. Each story is important to understand. And it also is important for each of us to take the time, understand the stories of all the folks who walk this magnificent country. Oh, just to give a little bit of background before we present quickly the first slide, please. Key elements of American culture.

Just before I begin to go into my overview. I like to make an important point, and that is when we heard from Eric, we were hearing from a person who has great ties to this country, and those ties are even longer than mine. My ties go back to the major European immigration to America between the end of the Civil War in 1865 and our entry into World War One in 1916. Importantly, we were actively solicited. We were recruited to come to the United States to help build the economy and to help fill the void where we had very barren population centers.

So our experiences are a bit different. I want to talk about some of those factors which many of the Europeans, both Asian and European, were attracted to in America.

So the areas I'm going to talk about today are the concept of opportunity, cost of opportunity, something that brought us to these shores, the mythology about American mythology that we bought into, the business of America. What is that? The concept of American exceptionalism, which is a major draw, pluralism, the role of education, and an element of capitalism called creative destruction.

In terms of opportunity, what we bought into was the concept of what was promised in our Declaration of Independence and our Constitution: life, liberty, and the pursuit of happiness.

Later at the beginning of World War Two, four freedoms were proclaimed by the president of the United States and the prime minister of Britain on why this war was being fought. We were fighting for the freedom of speech, of worship. Freedom from want, freedom from fear.

Now, one of the prevailing myths that we have in America is the Horatio Alger myth, and many European immigrants were introduced to this before deciding to migrate. The concept of going from rags to riches.

In Europe, the land was scarce. You could inherit, most people did that, they were tied to the land. Serfdom had only been eliminated in parts of Europe by the 19th century. So people still had those memories.

And Europeans of Jewish persuasion were limited in parts of Russia where they can live. They were limited to a place called the pond. So the idea of freedom, of movement, of the ability to have your destiny is very, very appealing. So the process was from Horatio Alger, you could be a poor boy or woman. You lead an exemplary life. You struggle valiantly against poverty and adversity, and then you gain wealth and honor and you realize the American dream. That was the concept, whether it was fulfilled or not, is a different story.

As Eric pointed out, that was not available to everyone.

Ok, now, once upon a time, we had a president of the United States. His name was Calvin Coolidge. They say that they call him Silent Cal. And a reporter supposedly once asked a question and said, Mr. President. I was informed that I will win a bet if I can have you speak more than three words, the president smiled at him and said, you lose. But he did say something is very important. When asked, what is the business of America? He said the business of America is business.

Now, this is a very strong and compelling idea for many people. For people who have experienced all of the corruption and issues with Europe, the fact that their lives were dependent upon who their father was, not who they were.

They needed a title to advance and be part of the aristocracy. We have a belief that the United States is inherently different from other nations. We are the first new nation to… take a look at history. There weren't that many revolutions until ours. We talk about, almost in religious terms, that we are a city on a hill that the Christian Bible talks about. And we strongly believe that the time at least we wished liberty, egalitarianism, individualism, republicanism, democracy, and Laissez-Faire. Americans have a, for the most part, a, not fear, but a reasonable concern about too powerful of a government. So we want our government to be very limited in power and we want to have checks and balances. We never wanted a king. We never wanted an emperor. We certainly don't want a dictator in the Roman form.

So we wanted to make sure we had a strong central government, but not too strong. A central government that can do things for us and also is one who does things to us. So that is embedded in our myth, in the idea of checks and balances and limited government.

There is still a longing for the rugged individual and being almost a pioneer family pushing the elements or levels of civilization. That's also in our myth.

We introduced this concept in the 19th century of pluralism. We even have part of our motto, E Pluribus Unum, but meaning from many ones, the idea of a melting pot. Immigrants coming from all over the world are putting into a melting pot and creating a new person. A new identity that is an American. America is one of the few countries in the world which does not grant citizens so much in terms of blood or sanguine but basically by where you were born, by choice. So you cannot say an American is American because you have one racial or ethnic group, American is someone who was born here, American is someone who chose to immigrate here and become a citizen.

And that is pretty much over. Oh, we have always been open to the Push-Pull migration concept. There were reasons for immigrants to leave, they were being pushed out of their native lands and America was always there to pull, pulling them here. At first, we needed cheap labor.

First, we needed cheap labor to work farms, then we needed cheap labor to work factories.

We had the cost of the chain migration, which is still in place today. You'll hear people challenging it. But that's, what's embedded in us. Someone comes over and gets a job, has an income that brings other family members over.

That's happened since sixteen eighties when we started moving for, maybe even before. So that's a bit in our history as well. So again, you'll see the crucible where America is. Or Columbia is creating the new American in that pot.

Now, this is from the 2000 census, as you know, we do a census every 10 years and we are in the process of trying to complete one this year.

And this is a map of all the counties in the United States and it identifies in each county what is the largest ethnic group as reported by the people who submitted the census. And you can tell from this that you can see concentrations of various ethnic groups in the counties. And you'll also notice that English and Welsh is not the number one.

You'll also take a look if you can take a look at the (inaudible) or the legend on the right-hand side, where you can take a look at various ethnic groups and you can see where they have settled. Now, in America today, we have many of these people who, of course, intermarried with everybody. Everybody marries everybody else in America anyway. But this is kind of interesting for people to identify their primary ethnicity. And those who call themselves American and quote-unquote, are part of a group called Scotch Irish, these were originally Scots who migrated from Scotland to Ireland and Ireland to the United States.

And there's one county here and only one county in the continental United States, which has a predominantly Chinese population. Can anyone tell which one that is? I'll help you. San Francisco.

Next slide, please.

OK, again, this is the concept of America being the melting pot, you have Chinese, you have Irish, Italian, Mexican, African-American, Chinese, Japanese, all going in one melting pot. It becomes America.

Ok, education, education was considered extremely important from our founding forward. We call for a free, appropriate public education. And the basic concept is that societies reproduce themselves in only two ways, biologically and culturally, education is the site of cultural reproduction.

John Dewey was an educational philosopher out of Yale University in the early part of the 20th century, and he gave us something very significant to consider, and that is what the best and wisest parent wants for his child, that must the community want for all of its children.

And this theme goes further. President Franklin Roosevelt said that democracy cannot succeed unless those who express their choice are prepared to choose wisely. The real safeguard of democracy, therefore, is education.

Ok, next slide, please. We're not going to review everything in this slide, but the idea is public education is a foundation for democracy.

It is the path to critical thinking, creative thinking, lifelong learning, and it also establishes relationships between parents, teachers, students, and the community.

The next slide, please.

This is a picture of a graduating class at Harvard University. This is an example of America.

Now, creative destruction is an important concept, It's inherent in capitalism In other political systems and economic systems, it's not there.

But in essence, it says the incessant product and process innovation mechanism by which the new production units replace outdated ones is the essential fact of capitalism. Process of industrialization that essentially revolutionized the economic structure from within, incessantly destroying the old one, incessantly creating a new one. In other words, in capitalism. One form of capitalism will destroy another, a more practical example.

We have changed technology. We remember that we first recorded music on wax, then we recorded music on 78 revolutions per minute desks, and we did it again with forty-five r.p.m. and then thirty-three, we moved on to (inaudible) tape, then we had a track tape and we had other forms of tape, then we went to CD ROM and so forth and so on. We're going to have some new developments. Companies that existed 50 years ago, many of them don't exist today.

Once upon a time, we had MySpace. Now we have Facebook. Someone somewhere is coming up with a replacement for Facebook, someone somewhere is going to create an idea and a concept which will eliminate both Apple and Microsoft. That is inherent in capitalism. One form will destroy and replace another. It never ends, is unceasing. And that's one of the things we have to prepare our kids for.

Our goal has always been to create a more perfect union, but we're not perfect, we're far from it on critical issues that we're trying to address today.

There's the coronavirus, COVID-19, and economic recession as a result of COVID-19, technology, innovation, and continuous or continual economic disruption or creative destruction. Needed job skills, and immigration disconnect. We're not looking for unskilled labor and we don't have that many jobs for unskilled labor. We have a shortage of people in skilled labor. Demographic changes. We have people who have been promised full inclusion since the day of our Constitution but have not yet received that dream. So that is in continuous flux. People are demanding respect for the opportunities they're entitled to. Still a process. We still haven't achieved that. Health care. Our healthcare system is unlike most other countries. Most of our health care is provided by the employer and the employer's plans.

Education. Education varies from one district to another, one school to another, it's not consistent, and climate change will be a continual problem. We'll talk more about that tomorrow. Nevertheless, we still face many critical issues as a society. It's like every other nation on Earth.

And next, the. OK, I'm going to ask you… I'm going to read this, but I'm going to ask you to do it on the next slide because it's in Mandarin. I'll say it in English.

Go ahead and pass it to the next slide. I'm going to end this presentation as I typically do. I would like to thank the Chinese people for providing America with the greatest gift of all. Your people. Since the very first arrival of Chinese Americans, they have distinguished themselves in every sphere of life. Without them, America would be a lesser place. They are part of the American tapestry, inseparable. The legacy binds our two countries together.

Thank You.

Headmaster Dave Delgado

Mr. Delgado, a graduate of UC Berkeley, has 30 years of private school management experience including in various levels of administration, school development and organization, multi-campus accreditation, quality assurance, curriculum development, teacher selection and training, student assessment, student counseling, teaching, and problem-solving.

Study in the United States

It's a good thing when I see that things are changing in the US over the last decade or so.

Parents are accepting the idea that children should not be pushed to learn but have fun and express themselves without the need for facts and I think there has been a bit of a mistake. Last year I talked about the basic info of highschool culture here in the US. This year with the couple extra minutes I have, this same presentation was enhanced to demonstrate my belief that the Chinese international students could be super students who could be powerful in the academic world. US colleges continue to provide expert education to students. Some of our lower education has declined with our elementary state schools or secondary schools not preparing students to continue to their state colleges. There has been a gap that is due to teaching facts or teaching concepts when there are false alternatives. It's like saying when you need to live, do you eat or breathe. You need both.

Concepts are mental space savers for facts But your mind does have to be filled with all these facts to base opinions and conclusions. This, I believe, gives the Chinese international students, whose elementary education consists of a lot of memorization of facts, gives a tremendous advantage when entering a US high school or college environment. If that student is prepared to manage the transition between the different education. It's a good thing to start with the factual learning and transition into the type of learning here in the US.

The knowledge is progressing faster than our ability to guess where it will be 5-10 years from now. Jobs and careers exist today that we couldn't have imagined 10-20 years ago and because of this, education and culture are evolving. We are currently preparing students for jobs that don't yet exist by using technologies that haven't been invented yet by solving problems that we know are problems yet. That takes creativity that requires a mind that is first filled with facts because some things do not come from knowledge. Every new thing is a synthesis from what already exists. The more facts you absorb from your early education, the more creative solutions you can come up with. An example of this would be if I am driving across a beautiful bridge, I want to know that the architect who built it applied factual engineering requirements before applying creativity to make it beautiful. The beauty of any new solution is built on a solid factual foundation. With this increase that is focused on science and technology and math and because of the wealth that has been created from that, the students have more options than ever in their core classes and electives. This evolution of physical sciences and creative problem-solving means that an even greater variety of choices in the curriculum is present in US high schools. I would like to characterize the high school coach in the US with 3 words. They would be the opportunity, options, and availability. On top of academics, another characteristic of American schools is the high priority given to sports, clubs, activities, by their community, their parents, the schools, and the students themselves. In addition, students and parents continue to want extracurricular activities. These would be characterized by our culture, community, language, leadership, government, media, music, technology, volunteering, etc. Public and private schools have contests in musical groups, marching bands, student governments, school newspapers, science fairs, etc. When jumping into this culture, there needs to be lots of quantity: do it all. The student who is the most productive, best educated, is the most desirable by college admission boards who will have thought through it and have the wisdom to think about which of these many opportunities that fit in with the puzzle of the life that they desire. The United States spends more per student than any other country, so with increased options and opportunities comes the right level of freedom to choose. That freedom comes with the responsibility to choose wisely and choose the options that lead you on the path to a successful and happy life. Fortunately, there are many resources available to American and International students on campus and off-campus. Do not be afraid to take advantage because it is there for you. The biggest mistake I see made by international students coming into the US is not asking for help. Many students are not accustomed to saying "I don't know" or "Where do I get help?" There are resources to help students do well on their academic subjects, selecting the right classes for a path to college, finding a successful balance for selecting activities. The students come from cultures where its all 100% work ethic and any learning disabilities or difference or challenge is not recognized as something that is a separation for help. Students that come here, if they are feeling depressed, overwhelmed, or just not like themselves, need to reach out to the resources that are here to help them.

I've worked with one of our graduates that went on to be at UC Irving to be a counselor and there were so many people that we're afraid to ask for help. They needed to be accustomed to the different ways that we viewed success here in the US. She went on to finish her masters in a similar topic to international education. We are now looking together at ways to help students who are perfectly capable but need to adjust to something different because the potential for success with the basic elementary education that they have is phenomenal. There are on-campus resources to such a wide range: counselors, advisors, faculty are there to help with scheduling, planning, and standardized testing. For preparation, there are not only on campus but also off-campus opportunities for help. With international students, there are ESO classes, test preparation, and just because of the type of economy we have, which is the quest for capitalism, if there is a need, there will be people to fill it. So there are tutoring centers and additional help centers everywhere that you don't need to be afraid to ask for. It is there for you, and it is very readily available. Free libraries, learning centers, tutors, are all available. Although international students study English, there will be gaps in their speaking English and they will learn quickly from their new friends. One of the things that I love most about highschool is the chance to mix American students with students that have left their home, their country, their comfort zones to live with sometimes strangers or distant relatives. That is also an example and an inspiration for the students that are coming together to form a wonderful symbiotic relationship. As administrators, we love to see that type of thing happening. Not only the academic life where international students are caught in the mix, but international students are also an integral part of the social life on campus as well. I love to see this type of learning or progress or any type of learning but international students can learn about American culture from textbooks but there is a better way. International students learn about new cultures from their new friends, sports events, dances, malls, movies, etc. American students learn more about other cultures from their new friends than they possibly could from their books. Even within the same culture, adults and teenagers use words differently. In the small campus high school culture where we are bringing international students from all over the world, we see such a great example of American culture that brings all sorts of different people together. They make good friends and imagine if they go on a business trip and remember that you already have friends there to visit. It is a beautiful thing later in life to have friends in contact all over the world. One of our graduates who was back in his home country in Australia posted a picture of his students from his class at school who wanted to see each other even though they were so far away in the world. To see them getting this understanding of the other cultures that didn't just come from TV, a book is so inspiring.

I encourage students to continue to go from one country to another to learn the cultural difference. I'm just talking about America from this point of view but the key to being successful is learning about the cultural differences when you are going somewhere new. It is an ideal opportunity to make a smooth transition if you go to a high school in the US and it gives you time to make that big jump into college. But the highest value that I see is that the students are building bridges from multiple cultures for future generations. Our governments may come and go along with the problems that are tied with them, but the people in education form bonds that far outlast that and go on forever. I do believe that the importance of education is greater than the freedom of speech, albeit that both are necessities of expressing our thoughts and feelings about. [Education] is what will continue to push society in the right direction.

Serena Mao

Serena is a senior at Mission San Jose High School. She competes in her high school debate team and participates in an all-girls robotics team. She also likes to experiment and create new things through arts and programming. In her free time, she enjoys dancing, hanging out with friends, and listening to music

Debate

If I was interviewing you right now about your political views. What would your instinctual reaction be? If I asked you if you supported M4A, what would you say? Do you support universal background checks for guns? Do you support ending arms sales to Saudi Arabia to stop the war in Yemen?

If you answered yes or no to any of those questions, how much time have you dedicated to researching those issues and forming that opinion? Do you consider yourself educated? Where are you getting your information from? Google? What pops on social media? What do you hear people say around you? Let's switch gears for a second and talk about debate.

I compete in public forum, a competitive high school debate format centered around discussing current events. Debaters typically spend 50+ hrs on research each month and around 15 hours debating on a single policy issue. Crucially, sides are assigned randomly, meaning we need to be prepared to win no matter what side we are defending. Debaters usually start the topic thinking "oh, this topic is super unfair, it's so side skewed" because we already have some predetermined opinion even though we really know so little about the matter at hand. Contrastingly, once we finish that month-long topic, we often end up wondering which side is true because we've explored both sides so extensively we don't know which we would support in the real world. To further emphasize the controversiality of these topics, even though judges come from super diverse backgrounds, the win rates of the pro and con are always nearly a 50/50 split.

It turns out that when you have a vested interest in finding equal ground for both sides because you need to win no matter what side you're on, suddenly, you see things in a totally different light. Usually, what we do in the real world is take a side and then research only arguments that benefit that side. We rarely give our "opponents" opinions a chance to win over. We've automatically dismissed them. We rarely start off neutral and then do research and then make a decision. Thus, clearly nonbiased education is crucial to allowing us to adopt an objective of a perspective as possible. Even though our gut check reaction should be neutral, we often already have an opinion from the start. In studies where people are polled on political opinions, even if people don't go in with a stance they will just take a side on the fly as they are asked questions. We love to just have a position on something or start arguing about something even before knowing much about it.

There's a pretty famous quote that reads; The hottest places in hell are reserved for those that remain neutral in times of moral crises. But this begs the question: should we really be obligated to take a stance even if we do not have adequate education about it?

Overall, we need to be more careful about taking sides, and maintain neutrality if we're not educated. Immediately choosing a stance, especially based on party lines, just creates an echo chamber. It's not productive if you just parrot the same things you've been hearing from people who already share your political standpoint. We're not educated if we just read biased media from your political party. You need to be educated on both sides of the issue, and not dismiss the other party or other side immediately as wrong. In a time where America is becoming increasingly polarized, we need to make sure we're evolving correctly in response to these changes. We can't just contribute to the divisiveness, instead, we need to reach across party lines to actually make progress.

Alice Zhong

Alice Zhong is a rising senior who attends Carlmont High School in Belmont, California. She enjoys reading, baking, math, and learning new things.

High School Cultures

Each country has a unique way of its college system. However, China and the United States do not share any similarities, and each has its pros and cons. While in America attending high school is a right, in China children are required to take an exam in order to get into their preferred high schools. Students can attempt to obtain higher education by passing entrance exams, which asks questions from a multitude of subjects and uses the final scores to rank and file students to different institutions. The Senior High School Entrance Exams (Zhongkao) make students face rigorous problems and are generally what determines which schools students end up attending. Applicants set preferences beforehand, where they rank which schools they wish to attend, and are offered admission based on their scores.

Seeking a college education in China is a similar process. While teenagers in the US are graded holistically based on a multitude of factors—extracurricular activities, volunteer practices, GPA, SAT or ACT test scores, essays, potential contributions to the college environment. Students in China are mostly graded on a standardized national exam. The National Higher Education Entrance Examination, called Gaokao, operates similarly and is hosted nationwide on June 7th. Although each student experiences some difference over what they're being assessed based on their province, three main categories are a must for all: literature, mathematics, and foreign language (typically English). The students are accepted based on the universities they express interest in, the threshold for the admittance of these said universities, and the students' test results. Applying as "Undecided" into college, although a common practice amongst American teens, is usually unheard of in China. The majority of colleges in China require students to declare a major in Humanities or the Sciences instead of having them declare after completing prerequisite course work.

Due to the significance of the Gaokao's test scores, students would often be extremely pressured before the exam. The fact that there is only one try on the exam and the tests were only happening in several days, the possibility for a student to not do as well as they normally do on the exam is high. In the United States, getting into a college was determined by multiple factors, that provide the student with a more fair environment. However, there were many pros in there as well. School shooting cases happen more often in recent years which makes campus safety a big issue. Yet, not every student can have time to do the outside activity and have money to purchase prep books and the standardized test, which puts the students from wealthy families at a disadvantage. Thus, there are pros and cons in both countries' education systems, but both systems have provided students an almost equal opportunity to present themselves and change their life.

Yukiko (ZhuoTong) Xian

Yukiko Xian is an 18-year-old student from China. She is studying at Los Gatos High School. She has participated in many activities such as Youth International Environment Protection Awareness and HEARTS. She also is a leader of the iCare Club.

Response of the Chinese people during the Covid- 19 pandemic

Preface:

Since the beginning of 2020, the newly unique Coronavirus has impacted badly throughout the whole world. We are all facing a financial crisis. In the end, most of the countries are expressing praise and support towards how China handles this epidemic properly.

So today I would like to share with you the strategies on how to handling this epidemic

The reason why we are successful mainly because we do have a structure administrative system and unity spirit

Through this anti-epidemic, a strongly built structure plays an important role in succeeding in this outbreak. This system has pulled everyone to work together towards the challenge, so everyone obeys the rules and follows the public regulations. Meanwhile, we do have: "ming yun yu gong, tian xia yi jia" which means our future ties together, we should always act like a family. Taking the action and the responsibilities for the whole wide world and all citizens, we have proved that unity has significantly prevented us from suffering and leading us to a bright future ahead of us.

Action now really matters!

We all believe that the earlier we take action, the earlier we can prevent the virus from spreading. In less than 2 hours, there are 300 medical support teams from different cities come together as a team: from gathering until arriving in Wuhan, average, not more than 24 hours, the mask production from forty-three hundred to 1.1 billion in 9 days, Huoshen Shan and Leishen Shan medical facilities has been built into use in less than 2 weeks. What a miracle production in China!

Quarantine has proved that it's a unique method to fight against the Coronavirus

Wuhan has set an example of locking down. The top international science magazine has published an article about the data: cutting down the case in a percentage of 96, 740 thousand people are anti-infective. China chose to sacrifice the development of the economy in order to protect the health and safety of each individual (including people from foreign countries who resident in China). We all believe that this precaution has a meaningful experiment through this practice.

Data, artificial intelligence, and cloud computing has served all over the cities in China

Manual temperature testing, overly costly of the vaccine research and development, supporting the administrative precaution, has come to the front line during this outbreak.

The discipline, unity, and the supporting spirit has played an important role in this anti-epidemic challenge

In order to take care of each citizen's safety, China has implemented the 24 hours lockdown administration strategy through the village, the community, and the district. Isolation is difficult, but from this, you can see all Chinese people have come together as a team in order to fight against the virus. Finally, we stop the spreading efficiently.

Beijing Strategy——the precaution towards the Coronavirus

Since the beginning of June in Beijing the Coronavius has arisen, we immediately upgrade the precaution towards the Coronavirus and arrange seven hundred million people to take the viral test. During those three weeks, a city with a population of twenty million people has stopped the virus from spreading. There are 335 people who have tested positive but they were all under control. We have zero cases at this moment, this has proved that we succeed in fighting against the virus for the rest of the world.

epilogue

Finally, I would like to share a motto with you: "He er bu tong, Mei Mei yu gong". What it means is the whole wide world has combined with all of us differently. And we should learn from each other. Whoever succeeds first, he might have better strategies for us to learn from.

"Unity" is strongly rooted in our Chinese spirit, and has melted into our blood. It has also represented obviously how we interact with international interaction. When facing a global crisis, we all need to stay together, cooperate together, learn to be understanding, and learn from each other. I hope we set a good example through our practice for the rest of the world to learn from.

Eventually, I strongly believe that the whole world will be able to walk through this pandemic successfully soon!

Eileen Guo

Eileen Guo is a senior at Gunn High School. She loves experimenting with various art forms, volunteering, and learning new languages. She strives to shed light on social issues that society has collectively been neglecting through her art, and provide a platform for the youth to voice their opinions. In her free time, she enjoys journaling, baking, and taking photos with her friends.

The Value Of Art

Art has been a big part of my life ever since I was little, but it hasn't always held the greatest value.

I started taking art classes when I was 5 years old, and it didn't spark much interest. Foundational drawing was monotonous and tedious. Resulting with a lopsided jar at the end of a three-hour class was definitely not rewarding. The few examples that I have seem a bit dull, as there aren't any specific stylistic elements in it.

I endured past foundational drawing and moved onto painting, and everything changed from there; I was able to work with color and something in me immediately sparked. From taking photos of landscapes to adding my own style into the paintings, color seemed like it opened up a whole new world for me.

After a couple of months, even painting seemed mundane. Art means expressing creativity and exploring beyond the boundaries; from ripping apart old magazines to plastic water bottles, to paper mâché, and pasting them onto the canvas to make a creative piece, the possibilities of art seemed endless. I have been able to explore with different mediums such as pastel, acrylic, collage, digital art, mixed media, photography, and make art with combinations of those various mediums.

One thing that most people may not realize is that artists have a voice that strongly resonates throughout all their pieces. Though art can be viewed as a beautiful picture framed to the wall, it can also be a platform used to express ideas and advocate for change. I've had the opportunity to bring past experiences into my AP art concentration. Through my sustained investigation, I delve into the growing pains and challenges the youth faces. Many people can attest to different ways they're hurting; whether it be the passing of a loved one, deteriorating mental health, stereotypes, racism, etc., the youth are fighting their own battles in a corrupt world.

Art has given me opportunities to find creativity within myself, provide a speaking platform for the youth, and advocate for change. It's something that truly sparks inspiration, and holds tremendous value to me.

Peter (Zeru) Li

Peter Li is a junior at Saratoga High School. He likes to read books, especially historical and mystery novels. Peter is a clarinet player in the Saratoga High School band, and he enjoys his time in the marching band. During his free time, he likes to play the clarinet, read books, and take photographs.

Individualism vs. Collectivism between the U.S. and China

Hi, I'm Peter Li, and I study at a high school in the United States. Today I would like to share my experiences and thoughts on the differences between Chinese and American K-12 education systems. In the past 15 years, I've attended many different schools, including schools both in China and the United States. I studied in China from kindergarten to 5th grade, then I moved to Irvine, California for 6th and 7th grade. Due to my parents' career relocation, my family and I had to move back to China during my 8th grade, and now I'm a freshman at Saratoga High School in the San Francisco Bay Area. The differences that stand out to me the most are testing, socialization, individualized thinking, and hands-on learning.

First of all, even though testing plays an important role in both education systems, there is a difference in how testing is used for college admissions. In the United States, your grade point average is more important than certain test scores. However, there is no such thing as grade point average in most Chinese schools. Grades for the whole school year are determined by the semester finals scores. Most Chinese people have a misconception that SAT or ACT is as important as the Chinese "Gaokao", which is a Chinese standardized test that is required of high schoolers to be admitted into higher education. In reality, these test scores are considered supplementary to grade point average, and their importance is less than that of the grade point average.

Now let's move on to the differences in classrooms. In the United States, students go to different classrooms for each of their classes. Making friends in U.S. schools oftentimes takes place outside the classroom. Students may choose who they want to make friends with and their friends don't need to be in the same class. For example, students at my school chat and discuss with their friends at the library. Whereas in China, students are stationed in their homeroom, and different teachers come to the class. Students in China study and sit with the same classmates every day. Students in the same class become friends naturally without any pressure because their friends are practically chosen for them. Students in the same class have a closer bond with their classmates because they are familiar with whoever sits next to them.

In regards to individualized thinking, the two education systems are at odds with each other. Students in the United States are given more freedom in thinking creatively whereas students in China are taught to memorize the correct answers to questions. In the U.S., students are encouraged to think critically and to question their teachers. In my math class, a student told our math teacher that the teacher's answer was wrong. Indeed, the teacher got the answer wrong but didn't get upset when the student challenged her authority. In contrast, students in China are taught to obey their teachers and not to question their teachers at any time. For instance, one of my friends in my Chinese middle school asked our teacher a question about a piece of history and was told that there could only be one interpretation. The teacher was a little bit upset because someone dared to challenge him. The whole class was a bit shocked when it heard that there was only one right answer to the question. Students in the United States are given more freedom in class to elaborate on thinkings whereas students in China apply their knowledge to questions.

Lastly, learning activities is also very different between the two systems. In the United States, students have more in-class activities where they interact with each other because they are encouraged to learn things from actions. It is more important for students in the United States to learn things through hands-on activities than getting good scores. For example, we do a lot of labs in Biology in the United States such as a pig dissection. In China, there are only a few hands-on activities in the whole school year, and students learn things mostly from reading textbooks. It is more important to score high on the exams than to really understand the concept through concrete activities. For instance, in my Chinese middle school, we did Biology workbooks every day instead of hands-on activities.

In conclusion, education between the two countries are quite different, and the major differences are testing, socialization, individualized thinking, and hands-on learning. Hopefully, in the future, the two systems can learn more from each other and improve themselves.

Arielle Yang

A rielle Yang is a Fourth Year Undergraduate Student at Boston University with a major in Psychology and a minor in Business Administration. In addition, she works as a Research Assistant at the Social Learning Lab at Boston University focusing on Children's Question-Asking abilities.

Depression

While we might think of depression as an ailment that affects us in our later years, it is actually quite commonly experienced amongst the youth. Despite being a representation of happiness and joy, the youth experience depression to a significant degree -- in fact, factors like stress and anxiety may impact the mental health of those in the age range 10-24 more than other age groups. Utilizing a 25-question online survey tailored to measuring mood and stress, we were able to develop a statistical analysis of depression with respect to stress and mental health resources readily available. With respect to our study specifically, three 25-question models were designed and released to anonymous participants that fell into our desired age group (High School Students in the Bay Area). Our questions were created to reflect our model on depression percentage which can be summarized as (Number of Girls Who Have Signs of Depression / Total # of Girls). The results of our survey and further analysis reflected a correlation between depression and stress/lack of mental health resources. For the Bay Area specifically, it was further confirmed that when compared to the national average for depression rate, the Bay area saw significantly more depressed students amongst our sample group. Ultimately, this demonstrates not only the fact that depression exists amongst the youth, it is quite prevalent. From our results and analysis, we can conclude that depression and mental wellness amongst students has to be reassessed as a serious topic. In addition, more resources must be made available to help educate the youth who may need help but may not know where to find it.

Ryane Li

I am a rising junior at Valley Christian High School in San Jose and have many interests in running, biking, table tennis, computer science, and not going to school (at least not in person). I have competed in F=ma Physics competitions and multiple hackathons throughout my high school journey. On top of breaking many school cross-country records, I have been nominated as the top freshman track & field runner in regional qualifiers in 2019.

Reintroducing Students to a New Online Life

Hello, My name is Ryane Li and today I'm going to talk about how students are being affected by their changes to education and how to reintroduce or rather reintegrate students into their new online learning environment. Before I dive into the issue of online learning environments, I want to give a brief outline of what I will be covering today. First, I'll talk about the problem that students often have when adjusting to their online environment and secondly, I'll talk about some potential adjustments in order to help students integrate into their new environment. Finally, I'll quickly go over who would be most affected by these changes as well as who would benefit the most by these adjustments.

What is the problem? Well, we found that nearly half of students find themselves struggling with their new online environment and this is due to a number of issues. Particularly the lack of in-person learning has affected teacher-student relationships and resulted in a decrease in student attendance/attention rates. This is caused by the increased number of students either becoming disengaged or distracted in class because of technical inefficiencies. As teachers develop their online skills, students also develop their online learning skills, however, a vast percentage of students cannot adapt quickly and effectively which is reflected in their school academics. Evidently, this issue of online classes is worrying to parents as they can often see a decrease in their student's grade point average and struggle to help students with their online skills. We find that students who can quickly adapt and feel comfortable in their environment tend to attend classes more often and see an increase in their academics and those who do not often feel encouraged to drop out and thus decrease class retention rates.

In order to combat this problem, I've arranged a 3-step plan to ensure that students will get the best chance at education in their online classes. First off, we want to ensure that students get to know their teacher as best as they can just as they could have during in-person learning. This can be done through personal meetings with students and their families during school hours. These meetings are also intended for families to plan around their child's designated meeting times so that families with limited internet access can plan for their children to engage with their online classes. In addition, teachers can record lectures in order to provide students who are unable to attend post-lecture education. Secondly, with their new online learning environment, a wave of technical difficulties has become apparent for both teachers and students. For students to learn efficiently and for teachers to teach effectively, there should be technicians in the classroom in order to provide assistance to any technical difficulties that students or teachers encounter on a daily basis.

Furthermore, these technicians are also in charge of providing technical support for the websites that teachers and students frequent for daily use. Teachers should also provide some guided learning practices where students can ease into their online resources and teachers are provided access to students' views where they can assist accordingly.

Lastly, and most importantly, an evaluation is needed in order to make adjustments to such a plan. With an evaluation, we can easily make adjustments in order to accommodate the changing environment or different types of struggles that students face. I would recommend that an evaluation of both the teachers and students would be conducted on a semesterly basis. This can be done through anonymous student/teacher surveys that the administrators could issue. With the results, administrators could make necessary changes to their learning environments if they conclude that a majority of the students struggle particularly with one aspect of their class. Lastly, it's important to note who would be most affected by these changes as their education is a priority since many will be deciding which college to go to or if they will go to college at all. For this reason, we decided to focus our ideas with highschool students. Additionally, we found that high school students were the most adaptive to their learning environments which allowed the greatest chance of benefiting the student population at target schools. With this knowledge, we saw that changes to the online education system were most effective at high schools at the local levels. With more changes in mine, a system of positive encouragement could be seen to be placed on a more widespread area if administrations were open to implementing such a system. I believe that in order to help the students with their uncertain and ever-changing circumstances, a plan of equal modularity should be implemented. Thank you for your time.

Yifei Huang

Huang Yifei, from Xi'an, Shaanxi, China, is a student of the High School Attached to Northwestern Polytechnical University. I love playing basketball, worship NBA Clippers striker Paul George, and also like collecting sneakers. I've learned new cooking skills. I'm good at dazing and killing time

Life During The Pandemic

Hello everyone, the topic of my speech today is the bitterness and joy during the epidemic prevention period.

In 2020, the pneumonia epidemic in COVID-19 will undoubtedly be the global focus. In response to the national prevention and control measures, all people will reduce their gathering and stay at home. Due to always being in a house with 80 square meters every day, no party, no community activities, and without playing ball with friends, I feel so boring and even my joints will be going to rust. Until I saw a friend sharing her flower growing process every day, I asked her, "Why do you plant flowers?" She replied: "enjoy my life." Thus I realized that this period of epidemic prevention and control actually asked us all a question: "How to live?"

As we know, many young people don't know how to live. They stay at home for a long time and do nothing during their free time. They have no work and study tasks, become idle, and have no purpose and no color in life. All activities they had can be included in eating, sleeping, and playing games. However, it is a waste of life. In fact, we have so much spare time that we didn't have before. We can read books that we are eager, try new things that we have never touched before, and finally have time to accompany our families sincerely.

For me, the 80-square-meter space is small, but I can do many things in this space. First of all, I learn to cook and make steamed buns with my grandmother, which is a traditional pasta art. What impressed me most was that my grandmother made a little princess and gave it to my mother. At that moment, the strong woman was also in tears. It turns out that my mother has always been a beloved little princess! Then, I read some famous books, which can lead me out of this narrow space and talk with more people. Moreover, I listened to Qin Opera with my grandfather, which is a bold and unconstrained local opera. I also learned how to make tea, because tea culture is profound and has a long history.

COVID-19 pneumonia should not only be regarded as a disaster but as an opportunity and a test, which is not only a test of medical standards but also an opportunity for us all to enrich our lives.

Aaron Zhang and Dillon Zhang

张时经 Aaron Zhang (G5, 11 years)
张时纬 Dillon Zhang (G5, 11 years)

How Can Man Achieve Immortality?

Key questions:

1. Why should we ask this question?
2. How to achieve immortality?
3. What are the benefits of achieving immortality?
4. What will we pay for achieving immortality?
5. What are the ways to compensate for these costs?

Content

1. Why should we ask this question?
   A few days ago, we passed a cemetery, thinking: if human beings achieve eternal life, then there is no cemetery in this world, we will not lose loved ones.

2. How to achieve immortality?
   – When a person is about to die, we use a technology that emits a brain wave to read all his memories and then copies them to a robot.
   – In this way, the human body is replaced by a robot, and the human consciousness will always exist so that the "immortal" can talk to people.

3. What are the benefits of achieving immortality?
   • First, the " immortal " can communicate with his family so that our family will always be around us and will not die, which is the greatest benefit.
   • Second, the "immortal" has a strong learning ability and comprehensive ability, the brain of the " immortal " to function instead of the human brain.
     – For example, when reading a book, you can write down all the details of the book in a short time.
     – give us a more comprehensive and complex knowledge system.
   • Third, the "immortal" has a stronger ability to imitate and exercise.
     – have a stronger ability to imitate and control the body, reaching the limits that humans can not reach.

4. What will we pay for achieving immortality?
   • One of the costs is that the "immortal" has a particularly strong athletic and learning ability, which can reach the level that ordinary people can not reach, so we will lose a lot of fun in the future-more than brain quiz, chess, and card games, etc.
   • Another bigger price is that our resources will be depleted.
     Because the dead will continue to become "immortal ", so that the earth's" immortal "species will be many, the earth's many energies may be exhausted.
   • The third price is that people may not be so close to each other for example, my father and I can get along for hundreds of years or longer, or copy a stronger "immortal" to replace my father, which may make us less treasured and less close.
   • There will be contradictions and discrimination between the immortal and ordinary people

5. What are the ways to compensate for these costs?
   • Solution 1 to cost 1(reduced human pleasure) and cost 2(resources may be depleted) are:

- The " immortal "is a robot, their wisdom and ability will reach a human extreme level, at the same time, human technology will develop rapidly, human beings will live on other planets in the near future,
  For example Mars, Pluto can even live on other stars.
- Solution 2 to cost 3(the distance between people is widening) is:
  - Write a piece of code in a robot to stop this phenomenon, and this "not close" feeling will not appear.
- Solution 3: the solution to cost 4(" eternal life "only increases and does not decrease, and conflicts arise with ordinary people):
  - The solution is that the "immortal" live on separate planets from normal humans, each with its own rules of life. When we miss our family, the first way is to visit each other by spaceship.
- Solution 4: to use another kind of high-tech, forced to derail the planet and move to a place very close to the earth, so that the two planets can operate very close together, with an aircraft between the two planets, Shuttle between the two planets at any time. However, this approach is technically difficult because the shifting of the planet makes the whole universe unattractive, and only if these problems are solved can the shifting of the planet be used.

2020 International Environmental Protection Awareness Conference

2020 Youth International Environment Protection Awareness Conference

Location: online; Date: August 1, 2020

Interpreters for Guest Speakers: Eileen Guo, Serena Mao, Zeru Peter Li, Kevin Zhang

This has been the sixth annual Youth International Environment Protection Awareness Conference. The purpose is to have professionals and students exchange information and ideas about what we can do to help the environment. We have translated, transcribed, compiled, and edited the speeches of all our speakers.

Proceeding Editors: David Zhang

Dr. Jay Jones, PhD

Professor Jones has a broad academic background, with concentrations in Botany, Microbiology, Chemistry, and Geology. His research and work experience includes Senior Research Geobotanist, conducting research on oil and gas exploration (ARCO), Naturalist/Interpreter (National Park Service), Remote Sensing Consultant (NASA/Lockheed). He is at home in the field conducting floral surveys, as well as in the laboratory working with complex analytical instrumentation. As Professor of Biology and Biochemistry, Jay has taught an exceptionally broad range of courses including versions of an interdisciplinary course entitled: Toward a Sustainable Planet. Many of these courses have field components in which faculty and students see the global impact of the human species in various countries around the world. His current focus is on finding transdisciplinary paths toward sustainability.

A "Fall" to Greener Pastures

Thank you for that kind introduction and for the opportunity to address this important issue. There are many books, articles, and talks given on environmental topics. So many that we become numb to their content. Most people realize environmental problems exist but few in the developed world realize how serious and how urgent these problems are. Therefore, I approach this talk with a sense of responsibility to not only share basic information but to touch the hearts of those gathered here so that we may work together to take action and reduce the impact of our species. The current trends in the world are not encouraging. We are separated from each other and from the natural system upon which we and future generations depend. However, there is hope and we can achieve an even better way of life while improving the environment. Earth is home to us all: Our families, friends, and neighbors – Every human being. It is also home to all other known living organisms. This is where we all live along with all known life forms.

This seems very large and from the perspective of an individual, it seems like it would be impossible to damage the whole environment. But although the Earth is vast. All living organisms live within a few miles of the earth's surface and the vast majority of humans reside within one vertical mile of sea level. We call this thin layer the Biosphere. If we compare a cross-section of an apple to the earth, the biosphere would be thinner than the skin of the apple. Still, there is a lot of room on the earth's surface and it takes many humans to cause significant harm. Most of us are aware that we are affecting the environment and that serious problems exist. The reason for this can be seen in this famous image of the earth at night. Each bright area is a city or another center of human activity. This well known NASA satellite composite was produced in the year 2000. Today it would even be brighter, with the growth of cities in size and number.

In 2000 the world population was about 6 billion. We have added more than 1.3 billion more people in the 15 years since. So what is the current state of the world?

- Human population has skyrocketed
- Scientific technology has allowed humans to greatly affect the environment and our ecological footprint
- We are using more resources than the Earth can sustainably provide
- We are also damaging its ability to sustain us through development and misuse
- The current course is not sustainable. We must change our ways.

It took 125 years to double the population from 1 billion in 1804 to 2 billion in 1927. It only took 13 years to add an equivalent amount since 2000.

We expect to have over 9 billion by 2050.

Science and technology have given us the ability to harness free energy and to create many synthetic products. As a result, we have made enormous changes and produced many materials that cannot be accommodated in natural environments. Plastics are a good example, and they are accumulating across the land and in our oceans.

Technology has given us the ability to use the earth's resources faster than the earth can replace them.

We started using more than the earth produced around 1980.

Today we use about 1.4 x the earth's productivity.

We are depleting the earth's reserves, just as a checking account balance declines when one withdraws more than one deposits. This cannot go on for long because we are depleting the reserves at an increasing rate.

At the same time, we are damaging the earth's ability to provide the resources we depend on.

Air pollution is one of the effects of our activity. Many of us live in areas with severe air pollution. It not only damages our health and deteriorates buildings and goods, but it also damages plants so that they are less able to clean the air and produce the food and oxygen upon which we depend.

Shanghai is one of those places but many rural areas also suffer from poor air quality because of mining or agricultural practices.

This dramatic photo shows enormous piles of coal. One of the major sources of air, water, and soil pollution.

Producing and burning petroleum is another major source of pollution.

Heavy metals such as lead, mercury, and cadmium are concentrated in coal and are released when it is burned. Most of the mercury in the marine food chain comes from coal-fired power plants.

Coal-fired power plant emissions can also contain significant amounts of radioactive nuclides.

We have all seen examples of severe water pollution. The upper left is one of the places on the Los Angeles River where the floating trash collects.

The one on the right is near Dublin, Ireland.

And the bottom left image illustrates fish kill due to agricultural runoff.

Dead zones in coastal waters

Coral reef deterioration

Groundwater and aquifer contamination

Loss of estuaries to development and pollution

Accumulation of organic pollutants, e.g. pharmaceuticals, pesticides, herbicides, heavy metals.

Salinization

Plasticizers . . .

Think bottled water is a good option? Sometimes.

But in our laboratory, we have extracted PET plastic water bottles and found significant amounts of extractable phthalates, which causes numerous health issues. Air, water, and soil pollutants travel around the world. Twenty-five percent of airborne particulates in Los Angeles on some days originate in China.

You have probably heard of the oceanic garbage patches in the five gyres. Plastic from around the world gets circulated and ends up on beaches and accumulating in massive quantities in the oceans. These toys released by accident over 20 years ago have now been distributed around the world. And we have also seen examples of the destruction of land habitats by mining, development, and agriculture. We are removing natural vegetation and habitat for mining, housing, agriculture, dumps, highways, and other developments at an ever-increasing rate. The upper right is a view from the Athabasca Tar Sands, one of the world's worst ecological nightmares. Pesticides and herbicides disrupt soil biota further damaging the ecosystem. Mining, industrial agriculture, construction, roads, airports . . . The animals and plants that once lived in these areas have no place to go.

The image on the left is a photo of the tallgrass prairie of North America. Over 98% of this habitat has been developed, mostly for agriculture. The image in the upper left shows circular green fields of alfalfa, grown to feed dairy cattle in the facilities shown by the arrows. The image below is one of many enormous piles of bison skulls created in the 19th century when these inhabitants of the tallgrass prairie were killed by the millions.

Deforestation is another example of the destruction of ecosystems to meet our needs and wants. The plants and animals that lived there are exterminated to plant soybeans, sugarcane, maize, canola, coffee, or other industrial agricultural products. Intense industrial agriculture imbalances ecosystems causing air and water pollution. One might also question the ethics of treating animals. I return to the fact that we are separated from the system upon which we depend. Few of us have experienced the stench and immoral conditions that are used to raise the chicken that we eat. We must reconnect. Chickens have personalities. Those of you that have raised them know this. Once you reconnect you will find it hard to buy or eat chicken that you know were raised under these conditions. To buy or eat chicken raised this way is voting for this practice.

Most swine are raised industrially now in a fashion similar to poultry. The average swine farm in the US has approximately 40,000 hogs. We would never treat our pets in this fashion. The rectangular pool in the upper left contains massive volumes of excrement, which contaminates the surface and groundwater. An increasing number of our vegetables are now grown by intense industrial methods with loss of genetic diversity and often sacrificed flavor and nutrition. The development of estuaries is particularly harmful. These are nurseries for many marine species. Aquaculture is becoming more common as wild populations of seafood decline. The concentrated confinement causes pollution and displaces natural habitat. The destruction of natural environments occurs around the world. These fields are in the Netherlands.

In the tropics, coffee often accounts for the displacement of natural plant communities and the animals that depend on them. My annual coffee habit requires about 5 square meters of coffee plants.

The result of increasing development is a massive loss of native and plant and animal life. Several authors have referred to this as the sixth extinction, in comparison with mass extinctions that occurred in geologic history.

Some suggest that what we have referred to as the "wild" will no longer exist.

On top of all of these changes, we are facing the reality associated with climate change. We must expect more droughts and floods, more record-breaking hot and cold weather, more severe hurricanes and typhoons, rising sea levels, and disruptions in biological communities.

This will decrease in agricultural productivity and increase the cost of food and other commodities.

Bill McKibben suggests the changes we have wrought have created a new world that significantly differs from the Earth we know. This is echoed by geologists who now recognize a new geologic epoch, the Anthropocene.

Simply knowing about the ecological problems often does not change behavior. I believe it is useful to put a face on extinction. I wish I could take all of you into a natural environment to witness the changes that are taking place. Let me try to give you a glimpse by showing some photos from a recent trip to Borneo.

Borneo is the third-largest island in the world. It once held a very diverse array of animals and plants. However, diversity is rapidly being lost as the natural areas are being developed primarily for palm oil production.

We can see some pie charts on the right that show the amount of deforestation. Less than 10% of the forest had been removed in 1950. In 2005 50% was gone. They estimated it would be 2/3 (~65%) gone by 2020. However, current data suggest it has already lost 75% of its forest.

Google Earth image of Borneo showing the position of the field station we worked at.

Flooding is common due to massive deforestation. The river loses about a meter a year due to erosion from floodwater.

Earthworms maintain soil porosity. They reach over 50 cm in length and up to 2cm in diameter.

Wetlands are vital for amphibians.

Small sampling of frogs. Loss of this habitat would likely result in their extinction.

Look at that cute face. Who would want to see this species go extinct?

This one is common in the preserve, this bear was in a zoo in Kotakinabalu but we captured several images in the preserve with critter cams.

This was the first direct encounter with the endangered Sunda clouded leopard in the field station. We happened upon it about 4 AM on our way to conduct a bird census.

Many birds including hornbills.

Along the river it was common to see macaques in the trees. There are multiple species of primates including macaques found along the Kinabatangan River.

I did not get to see these but my students were working with a research group and they radio tracked and observed their behavior during our stay.

This endangered species is common in the preserve and it is a joy to watch their slow foraging. They depend on the various fruits of the forest and would not be able to survive in a palm oil plantation.

This species like the Bornean orangutan is only found in Borneo. It is endangered and will likely go extinct except for zoo collections, by 2050.

This little critter is a Tarsier. It is a primate that eats insects and lives in the trees. This species cannot survive in oil palm or rubber plantations and has not been bred successfully in captivity. It will also likely go extinct if current trends continue. I do not have time to share the multitude of fungi and plants that define the habitat and provide sustenance and shelter for all of the animal species. Some fungi glow in the dark. This is a satellite view of the Kinabatangan River and Danau Girang. Note the encroachment of palm oil plantations. Deforestation has eliminated all but a few natural sites and these are not capable of supporting most of the species currently found in them. The prime threat to the survival of these species is deforestation for palm oil. Here it is very close to the Kinabatangan River. They are allowed to plant less than 50 meters from the river. That is not enough to preserve any large animals and losing 1 m each year to erosion suggests the days of this ecosystem are numbered. We passed many of these on our way back to Kota Kinabalu. This endangered species causes problems because they do not have enough room in the small reserves and cause damage when they move into oil palm plantations and other developed areas. We read about 10 elephants that were poisoned on our way out of Malaysia. The baby was dependent on milk and thus did not die from eating poisoned food. It remains with its dead mother. This species will likely be extinct in the next half century. Many food products contain palm oil. Buying palm oil drives deforestation. Look at the ingredients.

Most bath soaps also contain palm oil also known as palm kernelate. We tested the one on the right and it is one of the few that do not contain palm oil.

- First we must have a change of heart – we must care about others and the environment
- We must also realize that the transition we must make is a major one – a paradigm shift away from money and stuff to relationships and happiness
- Be assured that we can have a more fulfilling and "happier" life once we make the transition.

When we have truly embraced sustainability, the specific actions will be revealed in each decision we make. We must reconnect with the other parts of the system upon which we depend. We must think of others. Other people of the world, the plants and animals that share this space, and future generations whose fate will depend on the decisions we make. In spite of some opinions, the population must be stabilized and ultimately reduced. The red is business as usual. Yellow is the UN's medium projections and green is the UN's low projection. Just as important is reducing our individual ecological footprints. There are many ways of doing this. Lists help but the change of heart will allow one to see far more ways of reducing.

By reducing our numbers and collective footprint we can restore the balance of nature.

Good afternoon I hope you're enjoying the conference. More importantly, I hope you're finding it formative and more importantly than that even useful so we can take some actions. Now today I'm going to discuss economic and environmental issues, not the standpoint of a policymaker or a scientist. I'll speak from the standpoint or vantage point of a business person and an entrepreneur. The way I organize my discussion today is I want to talk about the tragedy of the commons, evaluate some market solutions, discuss a little bit about industrialization and externalities trade-offs in public policy, and of course no discussion of environmental issues would be complete without at least reference to global warming climate change and the green new deal. The tragedy of the commons is a parable but it's also a true story. A commons is a shared resource, it could be a pasture but there are many commons that we'll encounter at the beginning. We want sustainable use so we don't have overgrazing but since it is a common area and no one owns it there becomes a tendency for individuals to take advantage of the situation and then they will eventually deplete the resources that are available. In this case, they will continue adding cows until the commons become overpopulated and cannot sustain the cattle. There is no incentive to conserve the idea here is get it while you can; if we don't get it someone else will so we make a decision which benefits us at the expense of the commons. Now examples of the tragedy of the commons can be found in many many areas today. Greenhouse gases, overgrazing, non-renewable resources, population growth, deforestation, overfishing, and you can certainly add to this list. Now in developing market solutions we recognize that there's an underlying condition that we have to address scarcity. Scarcity meaning we cannot have as much of a good resource or service as we want at no cost. We have to give up something in order to achieve what we want. We also recognize that there are three types of goods: free goods are goods that are available without a cost at all; examples of that might be the fact that we have sunlight or currently clean air to breathe, however, the air that we breathe when we go underwater is not free, we have to pay for that and sometimes the sun becomes an economic bad which we'll talk about which we will pay to have less of. Now, most of the goods and services we encounter today are called economic goods as they are relatively scarce, and in order to have that we have to give up something else so there's a trade-off associated with it.

The third type of good is economic bads. These are things we will pay to have less of. For example, we will pay money to have less disease, we will pay money to get rid of our garbage and our trash, we will pay money to address the issue of crime. So economic bads are things we will pay to have less of. Many of the solutions involve something called private property. Those people who own the property have a tendency to take care of their property and it's a way to address the tragedy of the commons and in a market economy such as the United States, we depend upon something called the market mechanism. Buyers and sellers will determine the price. Decisions are not made by a central authority, they're made by the interaction of buyers and sellers at every level. Now let's take a look at how this tragedy in the commons develops within the United States. At first, we were 13 colonies. We became independent from Britain. we were very much of a farming, agriculture, and fishing based economy. Later we got into mineral extraction. When land became depleted all we simply did we moved west, ever westward, part of our manifest destiny. After we acquired the Northwest territories which is where Chicago is today, we purchased land from France. That was the Louisiana purchase and we sent Lewis and Clark to explore that later. We started to acquire other territories. They were first Spanish and then became Mexican territories. California, Texas,

Nevada, Arizona are examples of that. Later of course we acquired Washington, Oregon, and Idaho. Again, forever westward. We can't move any more west than this today. This image depicts the idea in the 18th and 19th centuries; a forever westward movement trying to try to achieve what we called our manifest destiny to occupy all of North America. Now, what were some of the reasons for our westward migration? The push factors included depleted farmlands lands which became increasingly expensive because there was a greater demand for them and an increasing amount of overcrowding, displacement of persons, unemployment, repression of minorities both in Europe, Asia and in the United States, and entrepreneurs who failed to look for another opportunity. The perfect example of that is the state of texas. the pull factors: we had private property. The homestead act. You can get 160 acres free if you simply moved westward and took the land. We had land grants that were being given. People were looking for opportunities; second, third, and fourth chances. There is an idea of just freedom being an individual and of course always always always, the sense of adventure. You can see some of the trails west, here there are major trails. The Oregon Trail, the California Trail, the Spanish Trail, the Santa Fe Trail. All of those were led by folks who had experienced the movement from east to west and immigrants were willing to take the risks and move and of course to get the land. You'll notice that there's a major barrier called the Rocky Mountains that is the second continental divide. The first continental divide was on the east coast and that was the Appalachian Range. So folks had to cross the plains and then the mountains in order to get to the coast.

Now, there became unintended consequences as usual. In the west, we have a scarcity of water and we experience frequent droughts. Our energy consumption went up, we depleted much of the wildlife habitat in order to make ranches and farms and homesteads. This resulted in the extinction and near extinction of plant and animal species. The land eventually became expensive. California is very expensive today. I'd like you to think for those of you who are not aware that once upon a time in California when the railroads were being built you could buy acres of land in what is now Palo Alto for less than a dollar, and the Southern Pacific Railroad and its predecessor the Central Pacific did exactly just that. And of course, if you live in the west you look at San Francisco, the Bay Area, you look at Los Angeles. We are experiencing overcrowding again. Now we talk about the business side of things. There's a concept in economics called tanstaafl: everything has a cost. The way tanstaafl is widely interpreted is "there ain't no such thing as a free lunch", everything costs something. Now industries are driven by cost efficiency and technology. So technology is a major driver where it makes something more available and lower cost for us. Our tendency is we're going to produce where the costs are least, we're going to sell where we get the best price and return on investment and we will look for capital wherever it is available including across borders. There's a fundamental problem here: not all costs are considered. We have sources of power, wind is one of them. The wind has been with us for generations both in Europe and Asia. We've had windmills of various sorts. They produced energy, they drove our mills, and actually pumped our water. Some of our will mills today are larger than the Statue of Liberty in New York. Water has been a traditional source of power. Before steam, our mills were driven by water power. Many of our factories were driven by water power. The steam engine revolutionized much of the action. In the United States what it did is it allowed factories to be run by steam. It wasn't dependent upon water flow. We could move almost anywhere so long as we had a source of water and a way to heat it and coal became a primary way of heating that water. So what did it allow? It allowed for railroads, it allowed for steamships, it allowed for factories and mint and also provided heat in homes. Electricity since the late 1800s has become more and more important. One of the challenges we had in the United States is that we recognize that because of the large capital investment and the fact that we needed a transmission and we could not store it the same enterprises which produced electricity also had the responsibility to transmit it. They were also given monopolies in areas so that we didn't have several different companies trying to provide their own transmission lines. Now today we're thinking about separating the transmission from production which is a major change from our approach.

Now there are always trade-offs in public policy, for example, coal. We have an abundance of coal in many of our states and for a long time, it would be referred to as king coal. Cities like Pennsylvania, West Virginia, and Wyoming have tremendous coal reserves but the problem we have with coal is that it pollutes. The burning of coal produces sulfur and other carcinogens and eventually, it will get into the water supply and the air that we breathe, and again we will be losing some fish and there's a question of health. This map shows you where our coal mining areas happen to be. This is extremely important because in the United States we have elections. Many of the people who are in these colored areas are in the industry, and if you notice in our last general election in 2016 these areas which are colored responded to presidential candidate Clinton's comments that we're going to put coal miners and coal miners out of work and coal businesses out of business. These people became very very fearful of their livelihood and they voted accordingly. If you'll notice you'll see conflicts between coal miners and environmentalists. The reason for the conflict we talked about shutting down mines but we haven't talked about what we're going to do to the coal miners, and of course if your future is dependent upon the income you got from coal and there's a discussion about taking away your future without any substitute that can be a problem. Nuclear power. Nuclear power is very interesting. Nuclear power does not cause global warming. Nuclear power does not have a carbon content to it. Nuclear power has other issues and that's an issue of radiation and leakages and how we are going to store nuclear waste. Wind turbines. We would think that wind turbines are going to be fine but there's a problem and the problem is that the wind turbines also are responsible for a good number of killing of migrant migratory birds of a variety of different species. They have caught fire there and now we have people who are objecting to the fact that we have wind turbines, and people will oppose wind turbines especially if they're in their own backyard. Now let's move on to a major issue, global warming versus climate change. As you can see it's complicated. Part of the problem we have is that it has become one of the most political issues of our day. Supporting the concept of global warming and the need for changes was Al Gore, a former vice president of the United States and the democratic party. On the other side the Bush administration with one of its major advisors Frank Lutz came up with a different concept. They said okay forget global warming, we're not talking about that we're going to talk about something called climate change. Climate change is something that has been with us since the earth was created. It's not a recent phenomenon so let's call it what it is, climate change, and let's discuss it from that perspective. Frank Lutz was quite influential, "Some people call it global warming, Some people call it climate change what's the difference?" The difference in the name was amazing. He also gave Republican candidates some ideas of words that they want to use. So first for example instead of using sustainable or sustainability, say cleaner safer healthier that makes more sense. Instead of saying ending global warming say solving climate change, instead of using generic code values, talk about principles and priorities, instead of saying groundbreaking state-of-the-art, say reliable technology energy, instead of talking about new jobs, new careers, instead of using security, talk about peace of mind, instead of talking about threats and problems, talk about consequences, and don't talk about one world - Americans don't want to be part of one world for the most part - talk about working together. Now the issue of climate change. Most scientists today will say much of the climate change is addressable by the human expansion of the greenhouse effect when the atmosphere traps heat radiating from Earth towards space. Now certain gases in the atmosphere block heat from escaping. Long-lived gases that remain semi-permanently in the atmosphere and do not respond physically or chemically to changes in temperature are described as forcing climate change. Gases such as water vapor which respond physically or chemically to changes in temperature are seen as feedback. These are some of the gases that we're talking about. In climate change clearly we're talking about carbon dioxide, methane, nitroxide. The atmosphere of venus like mars is nearly all carbon dioxide. Venus has about 154 000 times as much carbon dioxide in this atmosphere as the Earth, and about 19 000 times as much as mars does, producing a runaway greenhouse effect and a surface temperature hot enough to melt lead. On earth, human activities are changing the natural greenhouse over the last century. The burning of fossil fuels like coal and oil has increased the concentration of atmospheric carbon dioxide. This happens because the coal or oil burning process combines carbon and oxygen in the air to make co2 carbon dioxide. To a lesser extent the cleaning of land, the clearing of land for the agriculture industry, and other human activities have increased concentrations of greenhouse gases.

Scientists have looked at global change not just for the last 50 or 20 years but for thousands of years. What we recognize is that there were at least 78 major temperature swings in the last 4 500 years, including two since the 1970s. Now, much of this is about solar radiation, however that doesn't explain all of it. The most recent changes are actually the result of human actions. It's reasonable to assume that changes in the sun's energy output would cause the climate to change since the sun is the fundamental source of energy that drives our climate system. Indeed studies show that solar variability has played a role in past climate changes, for example, a decrease in solar activity with an increase in volcanic activity is thought to have helped trigger the little ice age between 1650 and 1850, and when Greenland cooled from 1410 to 1720s and glaciers advanced in the alps. But several lines of evidence show that current global warming cannot be explained by changes in energy for the sun. Since 1750, the average amount of energy coming from the sun either remained constant or increased slightly. If the warming were caused by a more active sun, then scientists would expect to see warmer temperatures at all layers of the atmosphere, instead, they have observed a cooling in the upper atmosphere and a warming at the surface and lower parts of the atmosphere. That's because greenhouse gases are trapping heat in the lower atmosphere. In its fifth assessment report, the intergovernmental panel on climate change, a group of 1300 independent scientists and experts from countries all over the world under the auspices of the united nations concluded there's more than 95% probability that human activities over the past 50 years have warmed the planet. Industrial activities that our modern civilizations depend upon have raised atmospheric carbon dioxide levels from 280 parts per million to 412 parts per million in the last 150 years. The panel also included a better than 95% probability that human-produced greenhouse gases such as carbon dioxide, methane, and nitrous oxide have caused much of the observed increase in earth's temperatures of the last 50 years. So what are we seeing? We're seeing changing rain and snow patterns. We're seeing changes in animal migration and life cycles. We're seeing higher temperatures and more heatwaves. We're experiencing more droughts and wildfires, especially in California. We're having ice melt or we're seeing the thawing of permafrost. We're seeing changes in plant life cycles, warmer oceans, rising sea levels, damaged corals, and of course stronger storms. Now, Frank Lutz, the Republican pollster and advisor to George Bush, appeared recently in front of the senate and his opinions have changed. He said, "I was wrong in 2001. I don't want credit. I don't want blame. Just stop using something that I wrote 18 years ago because it's not accurate today". He also said the focus is on the consequences of inaction, but the American people wanted to know the positiveness, not just the negative, not the fear, we want to know the benefit of focusing on it so. In summary, every policy decision involves trade-offs as balancing the interest of diverse groups is very very difficult. Almost every decision has winners and losers. The tragedy of the commons still applies. Not all costs that are externalities are considered and manufacturing will continue to be done wherever costs are the lowest. Thank you very much for your time and attention. I hope you understand that we're not focusing on the alarmists or the deniers, we're trying to focus on real-world problems and real-world solutions, and each and every one of us is part of the solution or part of the problem.

Mr. Carl Scmidt

Carl Schmidt is a Business Education teacher at Mont Vista High School in Cupertino, California. He is one of the founders of Silicon Valley DECA, one of three California Districts. He just ended his second term as Chairperson of the California Association of DECA.

Mr. Schmidt completed his undergraduate work in Economics and later earned both a Masters Of Business Administration (International Business) and a Master of Arts in Education (Educational Leadership). Prior to his teaching career, he was a senior consultant for Price Waterhouse in New York City and both a Manager, Information Systems and Materials Manager for Xerox Corporation's Southern California Manufacturing Operations. He also had the opportunity to serve as a co-founder and Executive Vice President of a Global Electronics start-up.

Environmental Issues

Good afternoon I hope you're enjoying the conference. More importantly, I hope you're finding it formative and more importantly than that even useful so we can take some actions. Now today I'm going to discuss economic and environmental issues, not the standpoint of a policymaker or a scientist I'll speak from the standpoint or vantage point of a business person and an entrepreneur. The way I organize my discussion today is I want to talk about the tragedy of the commons, evaluate some market solutions, discuss a little bit about industrialization and externalities trade-offs in public policy, and of course no discussion of environmental issues would be complete without at least reference to global warming climate change and the green new deal. The tragedy of the commons is a parable but it's also a true story. A commons is a shared resource, it could be a pasture but there are many commons that we'll encounter at the beginning. We want sustainable use so we don't have overgrazing but since it is a common area and no one owns it there becomes a tendency for individuals to take advantage of the situation and then they will eventually deplete the resources that are available. In this case, they will continue adding cows until the commons become overpopulated and cannot sustain the cattle. There is no incentive to conserve the idea here is get it while you can; if we don't get it someone else will so we make a decision which benefits us at the expense of the commons. Now examples of the tragedy of the commons can be found in many many areas today. Greenhouse gases, overgrazing, non-renewable resources, population growth, deforestation, overfishing, and you can certainly add to this list. Now in developing market solutions we recognize that there's an underlying condition that we have to address scarcity. Scarcity meaning we cannot have as much of a good resource or service as we want at no cost. We have to give up something in order to achieve what we want. We also recognize that there are three types of goods: free goods are goods that are available without a cost at all; examples of that might be the fact that we have sunlight or currently clean air to breathe, however, the air that we breathe when we go underwater is not free, we have to pay for that and sometimes the sun becomes an economic bad which we'll talk about which we will pay to have less of. Now, most of the goods and services we encounter today are called economic goods as they are relatively scarce, and in order to have that we have to give up something else so there's a trade-off associated with it.

The third type of good is economic bads. These are things we will pay to have less of. For example, we will pay money to have less disease, we will pay money to get rid of our garbage and our trash, we will pay money to address the issue of crime. So economic bads are things we will pay to have less of. Many of the solutions involve something called private property. Those people who own the property have a tendency to take care of their property and it's a way to address the tragedy of the commons and in a market economy such as the United States, we depend upon something called the market mechanism. Buyers and sellers will determine the price. Decisions are not made by a central authority, they're made by the interaction of buyers and sellers at every level. Now let's take a look at how this tragedy in the commons develops within the United States. At first, we were 13 colonies. We became independent from Britain. we were very much of a farming, agriculture, and fishing based economy. Later we got into mineral extraction. When land became depleted all we simply did we moved west, ever westward, part of our manifest destiny. After we acquired the Northwest territories which is where Chicago is today, we purchased land from France. That was the Louisiana purchase and we sent Lewis and Clark to explore that later. We started to acquire other territories. They were first Spanish and then became Mexican territories. California, Texas, Nevada, Arizona are examples of that. Later of course we acquired Washington, Oregon, and Idaho. Again, forever westward. We can't move any more west than this today. This image depicts the idea in the 18th and 19th centuries; a forever westward movement trying to try to achieve what we called our manifest destiny to occupy all of North America. Now, what were some of the reasons for our westward migration? The push factors included depleted farmlands lands which became increasingly expensive because there was a greater demand for them and an increasing amount of overcrowding, displacement of persons, unemployment, repression of minorities both in Europe, Asia, and in the United States, and entrepreneurs who failed to look for another opportunity. The perfect example of that is the state of texas. the pull factors: we had private property. The homestead act. You can get 160 acres free if you simply moved westward and took the land. We had land grants that were being given. People were looking for opportunities; second, third, and fourth chances. There is an idea of just freedom being an individual and of course always always always, the sense of adventure. You can see some of the trails west, here there are major trails. The Oregon Trail, the California Trail, the Spanish Trail, the Santa Fe Trail. All of those were led by folks who had experienced the movement from east to west and immigrants were willing to take the risks and move and of course to get the land. You'll notice that there's a major barrier called the Rocky Mountains that is the second continental divide. The first continental divide was on the east coast and that was the Appalachian Range. So folks had to cross the plains and then the mountains in order to get to the coast.

Now, there became unintended consequences as usual. In the west, we have a scarcity of water and we experience frequent droughts. Our energy consumption went up, we depleted much of the wildlife habitat in order to make ranches and farms and homesteads. This resulted in the extinction and near extinction of plant and animal species. The land eventually became expensive. California is very expensive today. I'd like you to think for those of you who are not aware that once upon a time in California when the railroads were being built you could buy acres of land in what is now Palo Alto for less than a dollar, and the Southern Pacific Railroad and its predecessor the Central Pacific did exactly just that. And of course, if you live in the west you look at San Francisco, the

Bay Area, you look at Los Angeles. We are experiencing overcrowding again. Now we talk about the business side of things. There's a concept in economics called tanstaafl: everything has a cost. The way tanstaafl is widely interpreted is "there ain't no such thing as a free lunch", everything costs something. Now industries are driven by cost efficiency and technology. So technology is a major driver where it makes something more available and lower cost for us. Our tendency is we're going to produce where the costs are least, we're going to sell where we get the best price and return on investment and we will look for capital wherever it is available including across borders. There's a fundamental problem here: not all costs are considered. We have sources of power, wind is one of them. The wind has been with us for generations both in Europe and Asia. We've had windmills of various sorts. They produced energy, they drove our mills, and actually pumped our water. Some of our will mills today are larger than the Statue of Liberty in New York. Water has been a traditional source of power. Before steam, our mills were driven by water power. Many of our factories were driven by water power. The steam engine revolutionized much of the action. In the United States what it did is it allowed factories to be run by steam. It wasn't dependent upon water flow. We could move almost anywhere so long as we had a source of water and a way to heat it and coal became a primary way of heating that water. So what did it allow? It allowed for railroads, it allowed for steamships, it allowed for factories and mint and also provided heat in homes. Electricity since the late 1800s has become more and more important. One of the challenges we had in the United States is that we recognize that because of the large capital investment and the fact that we needed a transmission and we could not store it the same enterprises which produced electricity also had the responsibility to transmit it. They were also given monopolies in areas so that we didn't have several different companies trying to provide their own transmission lines. Now today we're thinking about separating the transmission from production which is a major change from our approach.

Now there are always trade-offs in public policy, for example, coal. We have an abundance of coal in many of our states and for a long time, it would be referred to as king coal. Cities like Pennsylvania, West Virginia, and Wyoming have tremendous coal reserves but the problem we have with coal is that it pollutes. The burning of coal produces sulfur and other carcinogens and eventually, it will get into the water supply and the air that we breathe, and again we will be losing some fish and there's a question of health. This map shows you where our coal mining areas happen to be. This is extremely important because in the United States we have elections. Many of the people who are in these colored areas are in the industry, and if you notice in our last general election in 2016 these areas which are colored responded to presidential candidate Clinton's comments that we're going to put coal miners and coal miners out of work and coal businesses out of business. These people became very very fearful of their livelihood and they voted accordingly. If you'll notice you'll see conflicts between coal miners and environmentalists. The reason for the conflict we talked about shutting down mines but we haven't talked about what we're going to do to the coal miners, and of course if your future is dependent upon the income you got from coal and there's a discussion about taking away your future without any substitute that can be a problem. Nuclear power. Nuclear power is very interesting. Nuclear power does not cause global warming. Nuclear power does not have a carbon content to it. Nuclear power has other issues and that's an issue of radiation and leakages and how we are going to store nuclear waste. Wind turbines. We would think that wind turbines are going to be fine but there's a problem and the problem is that the wind turbines also are responsible for a good number of killing of migrant migratory birds of a variety of different species. They have caught fire there and now we have people who are objecting to the fact that we have wind turbines, and people will oppose wind turbines especially if they're in their own backyard. Now let's move on to a major issue, global warming versus climate change. As you can see it's complicated. Part of the problem we have is that it has become one of the most political issues of our day. Supporting the concept of global warming and the need for changes was Al Gore, a former vice president of the United States and the democratic party. On the other side the Bush administration with one of its major advisors Frank Lutz came up with a different concept. They said okay forget global warming, we're not talking about that we're going to talk about something called climate change. Climate change is something that has been with us since the earth has been created. It's not a recent phenomenon so let's call it what it is, climate change, and let's discuss it from that perspective. Frank Lutz was quite influential, "Some people call it global warming, Some people call it climate change what's the difference?" The difference in the name was amazing. He also gave Republican candidates some ideas of words that they want to use. So first for example instead of using sustainable or sustainability, say cleaner safer healthier that makes more sense. Instead of saying ending global warming say solving climate change, instead of using generic code values, talk about principles and priorities, instead of saying groundbreaking state-of-the-art, say reliable technology energy, instead of talking about new jobs, new careers, instead of using security, talk about peace of mind, instead of talking about threats and problems, talk about consequences, and don't talk about one world - Americans don't want to be part of one world for the most part - talk about working together. Now the issue of climate change. Most scientists today will say much of the climate change is addressable by the human expansion of the greenhouse effect when the atmosphere traps heat radiating from Earth towards space. Now certain gases in the atmosphere block heat from escaping. Long-lived gases that remain semi-permanently in the atmosphere and do not respond physically or chemically to changes in temperature are described as forcing climate change. Gases such as water vapor which respond physically or chemically to changes in temperature are seen as feedback. These are some of the gases that we're talking about. In climate change clearly we're talking about carbon dioxide, methane, nitroxide. The atmosphere of venus like mars is nearly all carbon dioxide. Venus has about 154 000 times as much carbon dioxide in this atmosphere as the Earth, and about 19 000 times as much as mars does, producing a runaway greenhouse effect and a surface temperature hot enough to melt lead. On earth, human activities are changing the natural greenhouse over the last century. The burning of fossil fuels like coal and oil has increased the concentration of atmospheric carbon dioxide. This happens because the coal or oil burning process combines carbon and oxygen in the air to make co2 carbon dioxide. To a lesser extent the cleaning of land, the clearing of land for the agriculture industry, and other human activities have increased concentrations of greenhouse gases.

Scientists have looked at global change not just for the last 50 or 20 years but for thousands of years. What we recognize is that there were at least 78 major temperature swings in the last 4 500 years, including two since the 1970s. Now, much of this is about solar radiation, however that doesn't explain all of it. The most recent changes are actually the result of human actions. It's reasonable to assume that changes in the sun's energy output would cause the climate to change since the sun is the fundamental source of energy that drives our climate system. Indeed studies show that solar variability has played a role in past climate changes, for example, a decrease in solar activity with an increase in volcanic activity is thought to have helped trigger the little ice age between 1650 and 1850, and when Greenland cooled from 1410 to 1720s and glaciers advanced in the alps. But several lines of evidence show that current global warming cannot be explained by changes in energy for the sun. Since 1750, the average amount of energy coming from the sun either remained constant or increased slightly. If the warming were caused by a more active sun, then scientists would expect to see warmer temperatures at all layers of the atmosphere, instead, they have observed a cooling in the upper atmosphere and a warming at the surface and lower parts of the atmosphere. That's because greenhouse gases are trapping heat in the lower atmosphere. In its fifth assessment report, the intergovernmental panel on climate change, a group of 1300 independent scientists and experts from countries all over the world under the auspices of the united nations concluded there's more than 95% probability that human activities over the past 50 years have warmed the planet. Industrial activities that our modern civilizations depend upon have raised atmospheric carbon dioxide levels from 280 parts per million to 412 parts per million in the last 150 years. The panel also included a better than 95 probability that human-produced greenhouse gases such as carbon dioxide, methane, and nitrous oxide have caused much of the observed increase in earth's temperatures of the last 50 years. So what are we seeing? We're seeing changing rain and snow patterns. We're seeing changes in animal migration and life cycles. We're seeing higher temperatures and more heatwaves. We're experiencing more droughts and wildfires, especially in California. We're having ice melt or we're seeing the thawing of permafrost. We're seeing changes in plant life cycles, warmer oceans, rising sea levels, damaged corals, and of course stronger storms. Now, Frank Lutz, the Republican pollster and advisor to George Bush, appeared recently in front of the senate and his opinions have changed. He said, "I was wrong in 2001. I don't want credit. I don't want blame. Just stop using something that I wrote 18 years ago because it's not accurate today". He also said the focus is on the consequences of inaction, but the American people wanted to know the positiveness, not just the negative, not the fear, we want to know the benefit of focusing on it so. In summary, every policy decision involves trade-offs as balancing the interest of diverse groups is very very difficult. Almost every decision has winners and losers. The tragedy of the commons still applies. Not all costs that are externalities are considered and manufacturing will continue to be done wherever costs are the lowest. Thank you very much for your time and attention. I hope you understand that we're not focusing on the alarmists or the deniers, we're trying to focus on real-world problems and real-world solutions, and each and every one of us is part of the solution or part of the problem.

Head Master Dave Delgado

Mr. Delgado, a graduate of UC Berkeley, has 30 years of private school management experience including in various levels of administration, school development and organization, multi-campus accreditation, quality assurance, curriculum development, teacher selection and training, student assessment, student counseling, teaching, and problem-solving.

What's in a Name? Environmentalism vs. Conservation

Good Evening, every time that I hear topics of environmentalism seems to focus on a high level or generic topics. I hear about every individual who should be doing their part in helping, and leaves the question of helping with what. Because so much of what I see would leave individuals with just "what can I do?" They can complain or protest or say something should be done, or the government should do something. But, no effective change, I believe, can really plan and enforce from the top down. So, my talk is a little bit different than most, I want to go from the bottom up, and from there you'll know what you can do, and you'll have a new way to measure the effect of what you're doing.

But, first, to say, I'm passionate about wild-life preservation, I support many forms of conservation across several countries, help animals like meerkats and cheetahs for example, and contribute all I can to multiple causes. Students at my school here have also gone out and gotten habitat restoration grants, so they're doing things to help restore the environment in our area. But I'm also careful about my words, I don't call myself an environmentalist.

Our resources, I think on some level we all realize, that this is the only earth we have, meaning that our resources are finite, or they're very limited. But in our own day to day life, it's easy to forget because everything really seems plentiful. Most of the time we are in good times, although we had many scares in the past, we realize we could be facing a crisis or shortage. We have an energy crisis, we have a population crisis, we have all these different crises that come up. The internet is growing too fast, but a new method technology seems to solve the problems, like stretching fuel efficiency, or new mining and excavation methods such as that, and life goes back to normal for us and we stop thinking about it.

Really what we need to realize is human continuity and advancement in technology have solved some parts of the scarcity problems that we previously thought as unsolvable. But still, I think it would be foolish to think that we could be rescued from wasteful practices indefinitely. What is the solution to this? I think there are two sides to the action we can take. Environmentalism is what we hear about a lot, and is basically the political agenda, the political activism that's pressuring our leaders into legislating solutions, making solutions that could be implicated on a large scale. These are the certain activities across countries, or across the world, that should be stopped or regulated. But the thing is that large scale top-down solutions involve extremely complex issues that really are beyond what we can speak of. But we will return to their important role in just a couple of moments.

The other side of it, conservation, is the core virtue that is at the very heart of the matter. And I want to define a few things very quickly. Value is anything a person will act to gain or keep. If you value something, an object more than the money you have, you trade to exchange one for another. You also act to protect things. Virtue is what gets your values for you, so conservation per se, if you value the earth, the animals and plants on the earth, then conservation is the virtue that gets you there. Really conservation is what we can do as individuals right now. I'd like to define conservation as the constant and ongoing effort to get the full value of every resource we consume.

Recycling is one of the well known well to conserve. It succeeds in its purpose when we get more value out of the plastic, the lumber, the metal, the glass…we can get more value out of it than we succeed in conserving. However, getting in your car and driving to the recycling center for a few plastic bottles is not conserving. By using a word like reusing and repurposing, it allows us to go to a new life cycle and get more value. Like recycling the plastic water bottle several times gets more value out of that. You don't have to buy a new container for that water. Say that you turn it into something else by cutting off the top and using it as a scoop, you are getting more value out of that same plastic. When you're out of ways to get more value, then you can throw it into the garbage or give it to someone who can give even more value out of it. So somebody who has the right equipment to get more value out of the same resource. Only a recycling program of the right size and efficiency is serving the purpose of conserving resources. To give a more specific example here, where we don't need the recycling center but will still give you the idea of creating more value. So, repurposing or reusing resources is one of the most direct ways to conserve. When I tore down this wall to make a larger space than I needed, I saved some of the lumber. Later I needed some stage platforms in our multi-purpose room. During that time we rotary our show used these large panels for several years until they no longer look good enough to display art. I borrowed the garbage truck they had been loaded on and delivered them to the school instead of the dump. A dozen boards would have cost me over $450 to purchase. The boards I saved from the wall would have cost me another $50 to purchase now. With a little extra work put in, a few hours of hammering and stapling, and sweating, new stage pieces are ready for our stage. I saved $500 but what does that mean? Oftentimes money gets so confused with evil profits or just the dollars. And I will explain what that means, money is basically just a placeholder for a value. When you get some amount of money, for one person it means more food, for one person it means new shoes, for another person it might mean a computer. So, through the gist of the action saving, now this amount of money ends up being free to use.

Education helps us to move beyond the individual scale to learn how much we can conserve when working together. Children are told that recycling saves our natural resources so it's a good thing to do. They learn to separate their trash when they remember to do so, and that is the last they see of it. They feel good about themselves, they know they did a good thing. They're not really understanding the economics or the concept of value. At this point, they are kind of learning a new habit. They begin to act usually in the high school level, like clubs that get started for the purpose of recycling and raising conservation awareness. And it kind of ends up being "well it looks good on my college application." So as an example, the student council starts a recycling program, it looks great on their college applications but nobody remembers to supervise the filling cans. Finally, they load all the leaking bags into Calvin's BMW, and they take it to the recycling station and get $10.13. At which point they start to realize the data doesn't show that they're getting more value out of it. Very quickly the idea ends up in disappointment. It cost $25 to clean out Calvin's vehicle that afternoon, all available data points say it wasn't worth it, they did a nice thing but it didn't create more value. The student council program stops and the student council forgets to tell everyone that the recycling program ended. And the janitor is left with the leaking, overfilled recycling containers at the summer break. At the college level, we finally have some scientific backing to sustainability. Because to start the program there is enough community participation to keep it going. It's supported by scientific research studies and communication. Now in these college-level programs, they understand the economics and bigger picture and now the available data points start to say they are creating more value than it costs. Because a University campus is like a self-contained city, that has students in science who get credit for doing research, groups, and organizations on campus that take active roles in sustainability programs and then scientific research provides the statistics to show if it is effective. Anybody who is more interested can look up the Stanford example. It is actually a good example of a university solid program, it's large enough to show results but not too large to study and manage how it works. It's being set by educated people and is supported by scientific research. To answer the question of does it conserve resources or does it waste other resources, the research from Stanford showed that even with the added cost it still costs less than finding, extracting, and processing new raw materials.

So what can we do in the meantime? To the fully developed University recycling system, with research and solid data to support it... What we can do now as individuals are to adopt and teach the virtue of conservation from the young child who's using the recycling bin to a fully developed college student. Our voluntary individual and collective efforts to conserve will provide models and examples that offer insights to our leaders as they work on a way to pull it all together. We need to educate on how individual efforts can conserve and create value. It is at heart for conservation at the individual and community level that is vitally important to our future. We cannot expect activists and the government to solve our problems from the top down unless they're met in the middle by our individual support from the ground up. Finally, environmentalism and conservation are two separate ways to solve the problem, and they will need to meet in the middle. The solution depends on all of us.

Jennifer Hao Ph.D.

D r. Hao holds a Ph.D. from the University of California. She is a senior engineer in Silicon Valley and holds more than 30 US patents. Dr. Hao has a wide range of interests, likes writing and reading, and actively participates in social activities. Served as the coordinator of all volunteers for the San Francisco skating competition for three years. As the coordinator of Hearts for 10 years. Dr. Hao also won the international Toastmaster English speaking gold medal, leadership ability gold medal, and was awarded the first place in humorous speech. In the end, she successfully nurtured three outstanding children

How you can live a happier and healthier life during COVID-19

Under Covid-19, everything seems different. No gym exercise, no coworker lunches together, no friends' parties.

Looking around, many people staying home are lonely without social opportunities and have difficulty purchasing living necessities.

The U.S. Census Bureau recently reported that a third of Americans show signs of clinical depression and anxiety. These and other mental conditions are becoming amplified during the recent pandemic, while COVID-19 patients and their families are also at high risk of developing depression and anxiety.

Experts predicted that Covid-19 and its variations will likely stay for 18 months to two years. How to live a life under Covid-19 is something we all need to learn. Here is what I am doing:

Find alternative ways: Healthy activities and Exercise

In the past every morning I went to the gym since the shelter-in-place order was issued, I have been unable to go to the gym. However, I increased my backyard planting capacities for self-grown vegetables and fruits as well as flowers. This not only provided my family with organic foods, but it also forced myself to exercise every day and reduced work stress so I felt happier.

Host Online Event in Real-Time

Every summer we have a trip for events such as providing financial support to 55 underprivileged children in Pucheng, Shanxi, bringing books to left behind students, donating food and necessities to special needs children, and planting trees in Tibet.

It's easy to say that due to Covid-19, we can not do it. But we did it and we made it!

1. Pucheng visit 55 underprivileged students
2. Pucheng visit left behind Children
3. Special needs in Shanxi
4. Third year planting trees in Tibet
5. GYLDE Competition
6. International conference

Connect with family and friends

Family connected via Wechat…. To have fun….

1. The first news today 今日头条（掌上新闻 ）

   Singing across the Pacific, Cloud Chorus Concert of Global Chinese Family
   http://toutiao.com/item/6844853269697659396/
   Singing across the Pacific, Cloud Chorus Concert of Global Chinese Family

2. Today's headlines (news focus)Today's headlines (news focus)

   http://toutiao.com/item/6844852061998154243/

Brian (Ruibo) Wu

B rian Wu is a senior student at Waterford School. He developed interests in nature science since he was young, especially in math, engineering, and artificial intelligence. He also has a strong curiosity and manipulative ability. He has participated in model aircraft competitions since primary school. In addition, he also loves traditional Chinese calligraphy and has won gold in the national calligraphy competitions many times.

Synthetic Biology and the Environment

The world is facing unprecedented challenges in securing a healthy and sustainable future. Habitat destruction, invasive species, and overexploitation are causing countless damage to biodiversity. Unsustainable extractive practices further increase the environmental burden. Moreover, rapid climate change is likely to expand the geographical range of tropical diseases, which will strain the already overburdened species and ecosystems.

Some of the approaches designed to solve these challenges have common strategies. That is, they rely on genetic manipulation of organisms to achieve new functions not found in nature. For example, scientists could alter the genetic structure of the baker's yeast to produce adipic acid, providing an alternative to oil-dependent production. Baker's yeast can also be reprogrammed to produce an anti-malaria drug called artemisinin. The application of synthetic biology is shifting from the laboratory to altering the genes of species for specific purposes.

The latest gene-editing tool, CRISPR-Cas9, has delighted the scientific community and the general public. It is faster, cheaper, and more accurate than any previous gene-editing tool. In gene editing, scientists use guide RNA to direct the Cas9 enzyme to precise parts of the DNA. The Cas9 enzyme then functions as molecular scissors, cutting or deleting the target segment. By taking advantage of the DNA's natural repair process, researchers can also insert customized DNA fragments into the broken bases.

CRISPR is now being used to repair disease-causing mutations, to acquire new traits in crops, and to synthesize new microbes. CRISPR gene-editing research is underway intending to alter the genetic structure of wildlife beyond human control.

With climate change expected to accelerate the rate of global extinction, the availability of CRISPR has the potential to accelerate applications for ecosystem restoration. Scientists have proposed using CRISPR for threatened species, such as corals under great pressure from rising ocean temperatures, acidification, and pollution. Strategies have been proposed to release GMOs into the environment to permanently alter entire target species populations as a means of eradicating disease vectors, eliminating invasive species, and providing resilience to threatened plants and animals.

Concerns about potential genetic cross-contamination, ecological interactions, and ecosystem impacts among species have not been well addressed. The current philosophical framework may not keep pace with the rapid development of synthetic biology and its inherent complexity. Balanced and inclusive consultative forums should guide synthetic biology and ensure that its environmental applications are used for the benefit of everyone in our common home planet.

David Zhang

David Zhang is a rising senior at Mountain View High School in Mountain View, CA. He is interested in physics and computer science and loves to learn new things. He is also eager to find out how the world works and why it works like that. He hopes that he can use his skills to help change the world. He does robotics, volleyball, and computer programming but in his spare time, he likes to read, watch movies and talk with friends.

What is Hurting Our Environment

The impending destruction of our environment is often mentioned in the news, and its extreme effects are widely known. The increasing scarcity of resources, rampant natural disasters, unhealthy air, destruction of habitats, and rapid temperature increase. As for the causes, we see or hear about vaguely factories or oil spills, and plastic items. Many would be hard-pressed to name the most intense source of climate change or the largest source of landfill waste for the U.S. Despite most of this knowledge is right at our fingertips with the internet, we do not take the initiative to find out.

To calculate the most intense source of climate change, a group of scientists considered both the energy intake, output, and scale of the gases produced in the process into a statistic called Radiative Forcing. This is a measure of the change in the atmosphere in regards to its ability to retain heat.

Although there are certain flaws with this measurement, it can serve as a general indicator of an activity's climate impact. And in fact(chart), it is transportation, not industry or production of power, which has the highest Radiative Forcing. This means it is currently the activity that creates the greatest change within the atmosphere in favor of heat retention.

One might think that landfills consist of mountains of plastic, metal, and processed material, when in fact, food stands as the largest component in the U.S (22%) and China(45%), and many others. Although food has a rapid decomposition rate it fills up precious space that could be used for non-biodegradable materials that require a landfill. Additionally, a vastly overlooked effect of trashing food waste is the release of methane into the atmosphere, Reducing food waste is just as important for the environment as is reducing other types of garbage.

People tell stories of mountains of plastic formed within the ocean and beaches that are littered with plastics. Although beaches certainly contribute to the mass of plastic floating in our oceans, it is in fact rivers that carry over 90% of to be ocean plastics and waste. Studies show that the 10 top-ranked rivers transport 88–95% of the global load into the sea.

All this is not to undermine the contribution of any factor which harms our environment, but to note their scale, and define their relative importance. It is pivotal that humans focus on the main contributors to the destruction of our environment. We must all learn how we can make the biggest splash using the technology we have or can develop, to fight the contamination of our planet not just diligently, but also intelligently.

Sources:
https://pubs.acs.org/doi/10.1021/acs.est.7b02368
https://pubmed.ncbi.nlm.nih.gov/20133724/

Kevin You

My name is Kevin You. I have just graduated 11th grade from Palo Alto High School. I have lived in China for 7 years and the US for 9 years. In China, I lived in Zhejiang province, Hangzhou city. In the US, I lived in the bay area in California. I like to play soccer, chess, and cycling.

Collapse of Easter Island

Today, I am here to tell a story. A story of Easter Island.

Easter Island is one of the most remote spots on Earth, located in the Pacific Ocean 3,750 km from South America and more than 2000km from the nearest inhabited island.

When European explorers first reached the island on Easter day of 1722 (hence the name, Easter Island), they found a barren land populated by fewer than 2,000 people, who lived in caves and survived from a few meager crops. However, explorers also noted that the island contained hundreds of huge statues of carved stone, which Easter Island is famous for.

Historians naturally questioned how people without wheels or ropes, on an island without trees, could have moved around these gigantic statues. The explanation, scientists found, was that the island did not always lack trees. Around 1000 years ago, Polynesian voyagers found this 160 square km small island, covered with a species of palm tree related to the Jubaea chilensis palm, a tall and thick-trunked tree. These trees easily grew 20 meters tall, some topping out at 30. However, when Dutch explorer Jacob Roggeveen first made contact with the island in 1722, he found no trees taller than 4 meters. Indeed, research reveals that Easter Island had once been lushly forested and had supported a prosperous society of an estimated 30,000 people. Scientists have analyzed preserved pollen grains under lakes and carbon channels in soils and found at least 21 species of plants, many of them trees. The island had clearly supported a diverse forest. However, tree populations declined eventually, and pollen levels plummeted. Researchers first imagined that the loss of plants was due to climate change, but later found that the Islanders have slowly deprived their island.

The Polynesians had unfortunately practiced slash-and-burn agriculture, where large areas of trees and vegetation are cleared for farmland. The trees provided fuel, wood, building material, fiber for clothing—and, presumably, logs with which to move the stone statues. The most supported theory is that the statues were moved with modified "canoe ladders. The methods that have worked involve using multiple tree trunks as wheels, along with great quantities of rope, which also comes from the fiber of trees. Thus, thousands of palms must have been cut down to create "ladders", faster than can be replanted. Eventually, the last tree was cut down, and the Easter Island Jubaea palm went extinct.

With trees gone, the soil would have eroded away. More runoff of rainwater implied less fresh water available. Erosion and runoff would have degraded the islanders' agricultural land, lowering yields. Reduced agricultural production then led to starvation and population decline Remains from charcoal fires show that besides crops, early islanders feasted on various seafood, including fish, dolphins, octopus, and shellfish. Analysis of islanders' diets in the later years showed that the people consumed little seafood. Without the trees, the islanders could no longer build the great canoes to fish and travel among islands.

As resources declined, Islanders guarded food, such as chicken, their main domestic food product, since theft was common. Eventually, the once prosperous and peaceful civilization fell into clan warfare, as revealed by unearthed weapons and skeletons with head wounds. Population declined from 30,000 at its peak down to less than 2000.

Well, this is quite a crazy story, as it might sound. Is the story of Easter Island as unique as the island itself, or does apply to a larger world? Like the Easter Islanders, we are all stranded in a closed system – Earth - with limited resources. The Easter Islanders surely thought that they were depleting their resources, but it seems that they could not stop, perhaps due to creeping normality – not addressing the problem because it occurs slowly.

Now, this so-called "ecocide" theory of Easter Island might not be completely accurate. Whether it be true or not, and whether how much it can be generalized, the story of Easter Island stands as a warning for what can possibly happen when a population consumes too much of limited resources.

Michelle Hua

Michelle Hua is about to attend her junior year at Evergreen Valley High School. She loves reading, especially science fiction and fantasy. She also enjoys writing and drawing. Michelle Hua is currently the editor of the health column for The Tempus Magazine.

Environmental Friendly Diet

Throughout the last decade, agriculture was responsible for 10% of the US's carbon emissions and roughly half the world's methane emissions. Agriculture has the world's leading carbon emissions and roughly half the world's methane in the last decade. The two main components of agriculture that contribute to this are the livestock and the crops.

The livestock are the most effective ones that contribute more so to global warming and climate change. The animals, especially on animals that produce red meat, such as cows, pigs, and lambs, are much more responsible for methane and carbon emissions. And, on top of this, they also require much more resources in order to cultivate a way, especially beef and lamb.

While crops are significantly less damaging than the livestock, they still do contribute to the carbon and methane emissions in agriculture. For example, rice, which is one of the most prevalent cereal crops in the world, the bacteria within the rice patties that break down biomass, creates a lot of emissions as well. And on top of this, both livestock and crops require a lot of land in order to grow. And while in some places, there are the farms already set, and many other places, there's still active deforestation occurring that causes a lot of the natural habitats to be destroyed. And on top of this, there's also food transport and storage, which further contributes to the emissions.

Because livestock is such a damaging part of agricultural emissions. My first idea, when I heard of this was that going vegan was probably able to be the best idea to reduce emissions, which unfortunately doesn't seem to be the exact case, since just changing your diet to a solely plant-based one isn't going to fix the problem. While just having a plant-based diet is beneficial, there are still other parts about the diet that will cause issues. For example, many vegan diets rely on lots of fruits, which might come from many different parts of the world. Many vegan people eat a lot of bananas, and I've also heard of, like jackfruit being a substitute for pulled pork and stuff like that. Unfortunately, since so many ingredients come from so many different parts of the world, the transport actually starts to make up for all the emissions that are reduced from switching to a plant based diet. And storage, similarly is also an issue, since there's a lot of energy required to keep all this food fresh. Like, if you eat any fruits out of season than that naturally causes more energy to be used in order to keep the food from going bad.

What are the solutions to this? To combat the transportation and storage issue, the best solutions to just eat foods are local, and in season. This way you help support your local farms as well as being able to cut down on emissions from both those factors. And on top of that, reduce meat consumption in general, because this way, while it still won't solve all the problems regarding the emissions, especially close to crops, it still does significantly decrease the emissions from the livestock industry. And of course, raising awareness. The more people that know, the more likely it is for change to happen.

The final wrap up is just to keep in mind the three issues that mainly affect environmentally friendly eating. Deforestation that occurs because of the need to expand farms for agriculture, the emissions that are produced or transporting the food to all our local supermarkets and such, and emissions produced while raising the products. To combat this, you can eat locally and seasonally to support your local farms that likely do not commit active deforestation, and this way to also cut down on transportation and energy that is used for delivering the food, as well reducing meat consumption to cut down on the livestock industry. While this may not be solving other problems in regards to eating, keeping these three issues in mind, while choosing what next to eat at a supermarket can help to reduce the emissions.

Owen Xu Li

Owen was born and raised in Mexico. He studies at the American School Foundation in Mexico City as an incoming junior. Owen is very passionate about Environmental Sciences and hopes to pursue a career in this field. Owen has also performed in multiple musical plays and in his school's jazz ensemble.

A Changing Climate Changing the World

1. **<u>Overview</u>**:
   a. Climate Change does not mean Global Warming. Climate Change is the change in global climatic patterns, like hurricanes, storms, and droughts in certain areas of the world. Global Warming is the average rising temperature of the Earth, which results in extreme weather, arrival of seasons and more. In short, Global Warming and its effects are known as Climate Change.
   b. The Greenhouse Effect is natural AND necessary for the survivability of all organisms on Earth. Humans are causing an ENHANCED Greenhouse Effect, in which more GHG are emitted into the atmosphere, causing more heat to get trapped inside the Earth and causing rising temperatures.

c. The Arctic and Antarctica are being the most affected since there is a Positive Feedback Loop. A positive feedback loop happens when a product of a reaction results in an increase in that reaction. In this case, when ice melts, it uncovers ocean water that is darker and, therefore, absorbs more heat than ice, leading to more melting.

2. **Impacts in the ocean**:
   a. Bleaching.
   Rising sea temperatures have caused the majority of the world's corals to experience "bleaching," a phenomenon in which the coral expels its algae. Corals have extremely important symbiotic relationships with these algae because these algae provide up to 90% of their energy. When corals experience bleaching, they tend to go white and shortly die and rot. This negatively impacts the environment since coral reefs act as ecosystems for more than 25% of the biodiversity in the ocean. In fact, coral reefs are believed to have the highest biodiversity in the planet, higher than rainforests.

   b. Ocean Acidification.
   Ocean Acidification occurs when CO2 in the atmosphere reacts with H2O and forms Carbonic Acid. Ocean Acidification causes the shells of organisms that grow exoskeletons from calcium, like corals, to dissolve or it prevents them from growing.

3. **Impacts in freshwater ecosystems**:
   Due to an increase in the air temperature, freshwater ecosystems warm up and evaporation significantly increases. This leads to a decrease in water levels and an increase in salt concentrations. This negatively impacts freshwater ecosystems because most animals are not adapted to high-salt concentrations and die.

4. **Impacts of COVID-19 in the environment**:
   COVID-19 has significantly reduced air pollution due to a shutdown of businesses. For example, in India, the sky was very clear for the first time in years. However, recycling centers are among the businesses that have shut down. This means that most single-use products are not recycled and more waste is generated, which means that water pollution and the number of landfills have increased. Additionally, the usage of face masks and gloves have increased water pollution dramatically as most of these face masks and gloves end up

in the ocean. In fact, scientists have speculated that in the future, there may be more face masks than jellyfish in the ocean.

5. **<u>What's next?</u>**
    a. Climate will continue to change throughout the next century.
    b. Temperatures will continue to increase if no immediate actions are taken.
    c. Due to increased temperatures, droughts and heatwaves will become common.
    d. Sea levels will rise from 1 to 8 feet by 2100.
        i. This will be achieved because the Arctic is expected to be ice-free during the summer before 2050.

Alisa Zhou

Alisa Zhou is a rising sophomore in the San Francisco Bay Area. Her favorite subjects are Math and Science. Alisa is a competitive swimmer and spends most of her weekends traveling throughout the state for meets. Outside of the pool, Alisa enjoys creating original dessert recipes, drawing, and traveling. Switzerland and Italy are her favorite countries she has visited.

Rapid Rise of COVID-19 in San Francisco

Since mid-March, there has been a major increase in Coronavirus cases in the United States, particularly in San Francisco. Coronavirus was first reported in the U.S. on January 21, 2020, and the first case reported in the San Francisco Bay Area occurred on January 31st. On February 15th, San Francisco declared a local emergency to caution residents to be more aware of the virus, even though there were a few active cases locally.

Two weeks after the first reports of Coronavirus exposure in the San Francisco Bay Area, two cruise ships wanted to dock in the Bay Area, but there were many travelers onboard who tested positive for the Coronavirus. As a result, all travelers on the cruise ships were transported to air force bases to complete a 14-day quarantine.

Throughout the rest of February and March, San Francisco was able to maintain a slower spread rate. In an effort to limit exposure, San Francisco recommended that people at risk of contracting the virus should limit public interactions, minimize travel, and all non-essential gatherings should be canceled. San Francisco went into full lockdown on March 17th, closing all schools, businesses, and public infrastructures to decrease the number of cases and exposure of the virus to residents. Health officials stated that the lockdown and stay-at-home orders helped prevent the spread of the virus, effectively flattening the curve so hospitals would not be overwhelmed.

Since the start of the pandemic in San Francisco city, as of July 25th, San Francisco has recorded about 5,787 Coronavirus cases, making up 12.9% of the total cases in California. According to SF Gate, the reason for the rapid increase of Coronavirus cases in the short time frame is due to low-income residents living in crowded accommodations, people ignoring social distancing rules, and community spread. A study found that in low-income communities, many households live together, which increases the chance of spread. San Francisco also has many essential workers in the healthcare and food industries, which contributes to a large number of essential workers contracting the virus.

As government officials started lifting lockdown and stay-at-home orders in San Francisco at the beginning of June, health officials saw a significant spike in Coronavirus cases. At the start of June, there only were only approximately 2,000 cases; now, at the end of July, there are nearly 6,000 cases, about a 200% increase. Health officials want residents to continue to be cautious of the Coronavirus and try to decrease the number of cases. The only way we can contain the virus is if everyone works together to wear masks responsibly and respect social distancing rules.

Works Consulted

Eby, Kate. "Coronavirus Timeline: Tracking Major Moments of COVID-19 Pandemic in San Francisco Bay Area." *ABC7 San Francisco*, Kgo, 6 Aug. 2020, abc7news.com/timeline-of-coronavirus-us-coronvirus-bay-area-sf/6047519/.

Graff, Amy. "Who Is Getting COVID-19 in San Francisco? Here's a Breakdown." *SFGate*, San Francisco Chronicle, 25 July 2020, www.sfgate.com/news/editorspicks/article/Who-is-getting-COVID-19-in-San-Francisco-Here-s-15428888.php.

"San Francisco County Coronavirus Cases: Tracking the Outbreak." *Los Angeles Times*, Los Angeles Times, 6 Aug. 2020, www.latimes.com/projects/california-coronavirus-cases-tracking-outbreak/san-francisco-county/.

"San Francisco COVID-19 Data and Reports." *San Francisco COVID-19 Data and Reports | DataSF | City and County of San Francisco*, data.sfgov.org/stories/s/San-Francisco-COVID-19-Data-and-Reports/fjki-2fab/.

Woolfolk, John. "Coronavirus: Is Bay Area Social Distancing Lockdown Working? Some See Progress." *The Mercury News*, The Mercury News, 31 Mar. 2020, www.mercurynews.com/2020/03/30/coronavirus-is-bay-area-social-distancing-lockdown-working-some-see-progress/.

Kevin Zhang

Kevin Zhang is a rising 10th grader who attends Mountain View High School in Mountain View, California. He enjoys video games, science, math, and learning new things.

Freshwater Pollution

My name is Kevin Zhang, and I will be talking about water pollution.

What is water pollution? Water pollution is harmful particles and debris in bodies of water.

Water pollution in many poorer regions around the world is very severe, and many people in those regions do not have access to clean water.

Why is water pollution a problem? Around 800 million people worldwide lack even a basic drinking water service, and 150 million of those are dependent on surface water. At least 2 billion people worldwide use a drinking water source contaminated with feces, and such contaminated water can transmit diseases including dysentery, cholera etc. Such diseases are estimated to cause millions of deaths annually. It is estimated that by 2025, half of the world's population will be living in water-stressed areas. Around 80% of the world's waste is dumped into the environment, polluting bodies of water and causing environmental damage.

What are the impacts of water pollution on the environment? Toxic pollutants released into bodies of freshwater can severely damage the ecosystem by harming organisms. Pollutants can cause algal blooms, where there is the explosive growth of plants and algae in a body of water, leading to a shortage of resources such as oxygen for other organisms.

How can you help alleviate the problem of water pollution? You can: dispose of toxic chemicals such as pesticides, bleach, ammonia, battery acid, drugs, and medicines, etc. properly, Eat more organic foods, which contain fewer chemicals that can damage the environment, Support and donate to NGOs focused on tackling the problem of water pollution, Reduce your use of plastic containers and products, which will not biodegrade if they end up in local bodies of water, Supervise your car to make sure it doesn't leak oil, etc.

What are the benefits of alleviating this problem? Access to clean water will be increased for people living in poor and rural regions, and the cost for governments to solve water pollution problems, in the long run, will be significantly reduced. The threat of people catching diseases from contaminated water especially for those without direct access to medical services will also be reduced. Such diseases can be difficult, inconvenient, and costly to treat, not to mention potentially fatal for humans. Less water pollution would also mean healthier environments and ecosystems, which in turn would lead to cleaner air, water, and food

Allen Bryan

I am an incoming freshman at Junipero Serra high school, an all boys school in California. I am interested in things involving business so I am hoping to create the school's first DECA club. I also am interested in stock trading and hope to gain experience in that area. I enjoy playing piano and hope to gain more skill when I play in the school's jazz band. I play basketball and hope to play football in the fall.

Drug Contamination in the Environment

How Drugs are Transmitted to the Environment

Drugs contaminate the environment in a variety of ways. Residue from Drugs can enter surface waters in the manufacturing process. Humans digest drugs and can excrete trace amounts into sewer systems which ends up in water supplies. Pharmaceuticals used on animals can be excreted into soils and surface waters. At any stage of life, cows, pigs, and chickens can encounter bacterial infections like pink eyes or infected wounds that require treatment with antibiotics. Examples of commonly used antibiotics for these conditions include penicillin, tetracycline, ceftiofur, florfenicol, tilmicosin, enrofloxacin, and tulathromycin. By using manure as fertilizer, drug residue can be transmitted. Unused medications are often disposed of into water supplies through toilets and landfills. Over 80 percent of America's streams have been contaminated by numerous medications according to a United States geological survey.

This is how drugs affect the environment, animals, and humans. Animals that consume these drug residues are harmed. Examples of this harm include the following. In South Asia, vultures have been poisoned by the anti-arthritis painkillers used by humans. In the USA, geese are being harmed from medicinal pills being thrown out into the environment. Also, drug residue has been found to significantly impact plant growth, some studies show. Medical drug waste has also been found in many of our waterways, being a huge risk to the health of humans as well as animals. Among the contaminants discovered: <u>bisphenol-A (or BPA)</u>, an endocrine-disrupting chemical frequently used in consumer plastics; methotrexate, an immunosuppressant and cancer treatment; and sulfamethoxazole, an antibiotic. This could cause sickness among those who consume these drugs.

There are also effects of growing plant-based drugs. Growing illegal and non-illegal drug related plants can also cause heavy damage to the environment. Cocaine and Opium production takes place in the South American forests, home to some of the most delicate ecosystems in the world. Plants and animals that could be helpful to mankind are being adversely affected. For example, many beetles that have value in treating serious diseases are being wiped out. There are studies that indicate blister beetles might be used to battle tumors and in chemotherapy treatments. Bees, with an extremely important role as pollinators, are being wiped out due to habitat loss caused by drug growth and production. Also, one of the major peptides in bee venom, called Melittin, has the potential to treat inflammation in sufferers of Rheumatoid arthritis and Multiple sclerosis.

Superbugs, bacteria with resistance to multiple antibiotics, are also being created. Due to antibiotic drug residue being dumped into the environment, bacteria, like those who cause pneumonia, urinary tract, and skin infections, are adapting to be more resistant to these drugs. After coming in contact with these drugs in the environment, they grow and natural selection creates superbugs that are able to survive antibiotic treatment. Medically important drugs, that once were able to save lives, are now not working due to the dumping of drug waste and general overuse. This has been called the next big problem of our century.

There are some solutions to this issue. Rather than flushing these medicines down the toilet, the FDA should change guidelines so all medicines are to be disposed of in containers given to people whenever they purchase medicine. This would be a safe place for expired or old medicine that is of no use. Not only should the FDA require this, they should also require these containers be pre-labeled for easy shipment to pharmacies for proper disposal. improper disposal such as flushing down toilets, or throwing into landfills leads to drug residues entering soils and waterways. Also, there should be stronger laws and regulations on the types, and amount of medications and antibiotics used for farm animals. There should be sampling and strict penalties for improper use and disposal. This way, there will be a reduced amount of medical waste found in the animal products, farmland, and fertilizer (manure).

Both medical and illegal drugs are harmful to the environment due to the carelessness of humans. Mankind does not seem to understand the necessity of properly disposal of drug waste which directly affects the environment that we are trying to protect. With new guidelines from the WHO or the FDA, we can reduce the medical waste found in streams and around wildlife, and protect the world, and humans.

Haibin Peng & Elaine (Yilian) Peng

Haibin Peng is a mature boy with a friendly manner. Being an upcoming eighth-grader, he is unlike others of his age (according to the comment of other people), is more obedient, and respectful towards others; also having an unusual dream. He is learning skills other than academics: Charcoal Drawing, Kung Fu, Chinese Calligraphy, Chinese Classic Books reciting are all his specialty. In the school year of 2020-2021, he will attend Basis Independent Fremont. Elaine is very dependent, upbeat, and loves to read. At her age, 11, she loves voicing out her ideas so that everyone can understand her point of view. Fun fact, her hobbies are dancing, drawing, and playing the piano.

Ocean Pollution

Good evening, everybody. We are Haibin Peng and Yilian Peng. Today we will share with you the problem of ocean pollution

Now you can see that there are many advertisements on the Internet that represent the same idea: the ocean is polluted. but it's not an issue that should be dismissed. Because the ocean is related to climate change and the water cycle. If the ocean is in decline, humans will also face the same. Finally, the most important part is that marine animals are dying.

There are many main questions on this topic.

Problem one, oil spill: oil spill can cause great harm to marine animals. It's said on the Internet: "Oil destroys the protection ability of fur-bearing mammals, such as sea otters, and the water-repelling abilities of a bird's feathers, exposing them to the toxic elements."

Problem two, pollution of plastics and harmful elements: Around 80% of marine pollution comes from land-based activities. Waste is dumped into drains, rivers and hence the seas. Oil, fertilisers, sewage, plastics and toxic chemicals are all part of the mix.

Question three, the death rates of marine animals are increasing: About 100 million marine animals die each year from plastic waste alone; about 100,000 marine animals die from getting entangled in plastic yearly – this is just the creatures we find! Also, 1 in 3 marine mammal species get found entangled in litter!

The importance of solving the problem: Our ocean is being polluted from trash and toxic man-made products. To reduce this we need to all work together and care for our ocean. As the article FA states, *"By 2050 there will be more plastic than fish in the world's oceans."* This should warn us to prevent this from happening.

The more important reason is that the ocean provides many benefits to humans. Such as food, medicine, oxygen supply, protection, transportation, and the two most important ones: climate change and biodiversity. These important points regard the whole survival of Earth.

Although ocean pollution is a big issue, there are different ways to reduce the problem at different levels. Individuals: Start from yourself: care for your own trash and be watchful of where they go. Also, we can volunteer or set up events to contribute.

Officials: Pass more restrictions upon the garbage system. Put more effort and funding into the garbage system.

Fun(but terrifying) fact: Recently, a news report found that there are A new continent with an area of 1.6 million square kilometers, but this land consists mostly of plastic waste from all the places, carried by ocean currents all to one place. Such an example is also found in the Mediterranean region. Imagine how much garbage we humans produce, and how it affects nature. Therefore, everyone must pay attention to the seriousness of the Ocean/marine pollution in the future!

This is our online resource. ---and Thank you for listening to our speech!

Nathaniel Guo, Chia-Kuang Tan, and Santony Duan

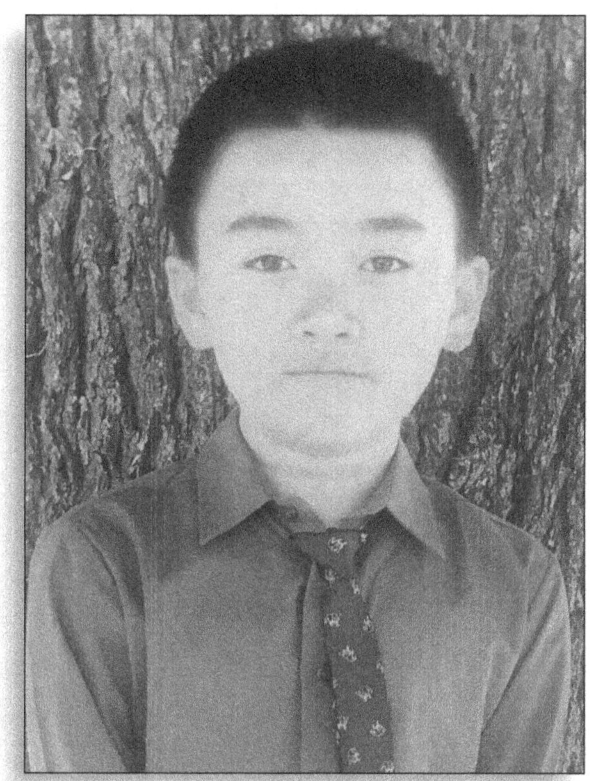

Nathaniel Guo

He likes dead memes and plays minecraft a lot, he has some interest in biology and other science related topics, he also likes the history of wars and other things like that. He likes playing tf2, minecraft and other things.

他喜欢死模因，经常玩《我的世界》，他对生物学和其他与科学有关的话题感兴趣，他还喜欢战争的历史以及类似的事物。 他喜欢玩tf2，Minecraft和其他东西。

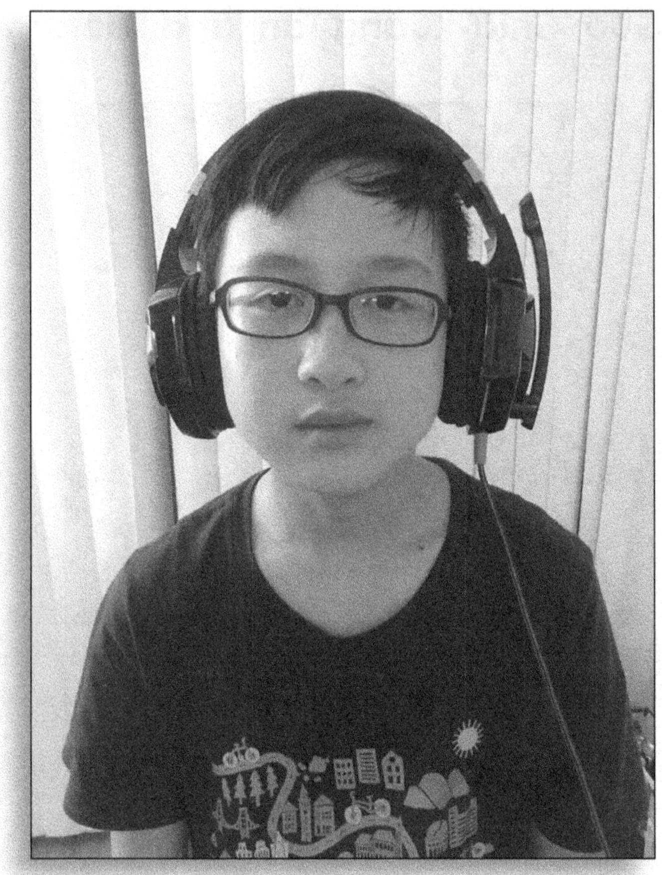

Chia-Kuang Tan

He is addicted to Rubik's Cubes and also would like to buy 7 cubes each 3 months for a discount of 30%. He has equally the same interest in all of the classes including history and math and science and Robotics and other kinds of things. But most likely he is going to be a car engineer by using all of the knowledge he has obtained from 1st grade. He likes to smash Rubik's cubes in his times of boredom or reading or playing Forza Horizon 4 and Minecraft.

他对魔方非常沉迷，对所有课程都同样感兴趣，包括历史、数学、科学、机器人及其他等等。从小学一年级起，他就想要成为一名汽车工程师并持续努力学习相关知识。课余时间，他喜欢将各种魔方拆解再重组来打发时间，也喜欢上线玩Forza Horizon 4及 Minecraft。

Santony Duan

He has an interest in video games, specifically TF2 and Roblox. Enjoys learning about animals, especially ones that live in the ocean. He also likes science and world history. He also plays basketball in his free time, and in times where he has nothing better to do. Likes hanging out with his friends like Nathaniel.

他对视频游戏特别是TF2和Roblox感兴趣。喜欢学习动物，尤其是生活在海洋中的动物。也喜欢科学和世界历史。他还在业余时间和无事可做的时候打篮球。喜欢和Nathaniel等朋友一起出去玩。

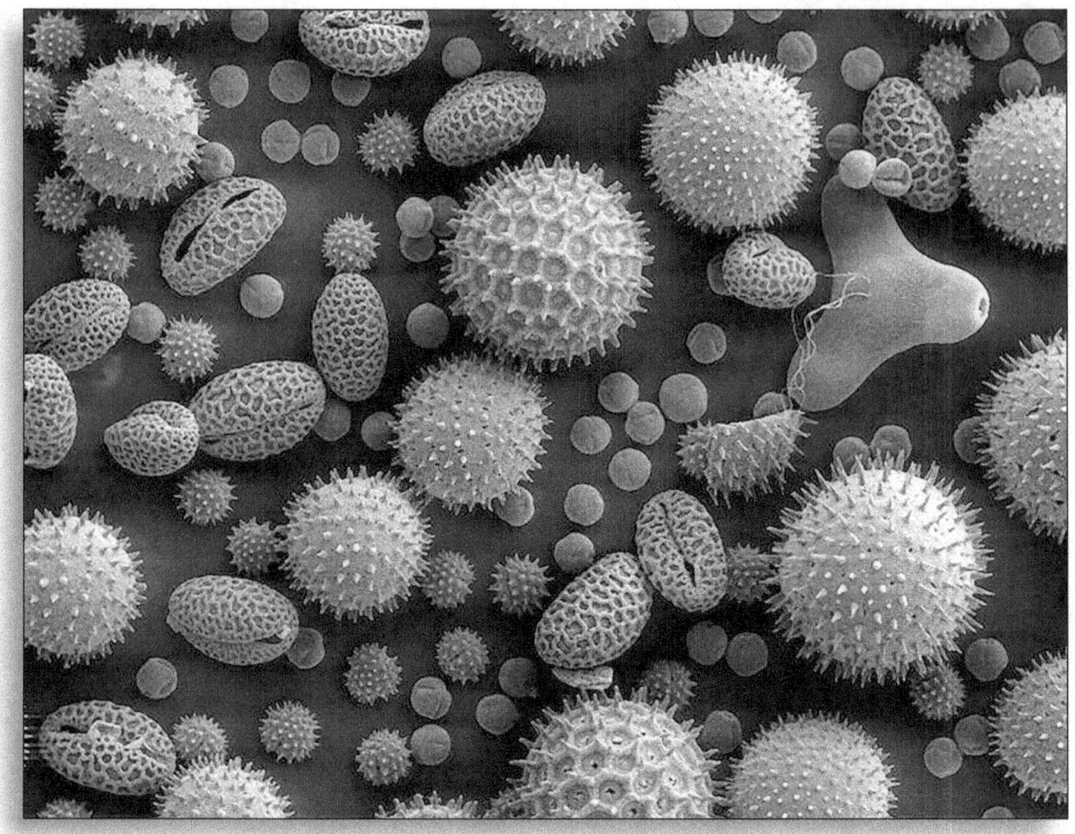

What is air pollution?

What is air pollution? Air pollution is known as the pollutants that are released from burning fossil fuels and other forms of energy production. These pollutants, when released into the atmosphere, have devastating results on the Earth and your health. They play a role in climate change, respiratory health problems, and contribute to other natural pollutants like acid rain and smog. Examples of air pollution include carbon dioxide, methane, and other greenhouse gases; smog, which is formed and worsened in heat, and mold and pollen, which are natural allergenic air pollutants that can be detrimental to the health of hypersensitive people.

什么是空气污染？

空气污染被称为燃烧化石燃料和其他形式的能源生产过程中释放的污染物。这些污染物释放到大气中后，会对地球和您的健康造成毁灭性的后果。它们在气候变化，呼吸系统健康问题中起作用，并导致其他自然污染物，例如酸雨和烟雾。空气污染的例子包括二氧化碳，甲烷和其他温室气体。在热中形成并恶化的烟雾，霉菌和花粉是自然的致敏性空气污染物，可能对超敏人群的健康有害。

https://www.nrdc.org/stories/air-pollution-everything-you-need-know

What causes air pollution

Air pollution is a form of releasing harmful air particles such as carbon dioxide and methane into the air and not including flatulence even though it also releases carbon dioxide into the atmosphere if it goes that far without being inhaled. Some of the most common worldwide air pollution seen in the world include mass amounts of energy use of greenhouse gas in many production companies such as fossil fuel usage. By doing those things they release destructive gas and chemicals into the air. Air pollution contributes and also becomes way more dangerous in climate change. It is bad for the earth because it makes warm weather drier and also generates ultraviolet light.

造成空气污染的原因

空气污染是一种将不良的空气颗粒（例如二氧化碳和甲烷）释放到空气中的一种形式。世界上最常见的空气污染主要是来自化石燃料的使用，许多制造业工厂使用这些会产生温室气体的化石燃料，它们将破坏性的气体和化学物质释放到空气中。空气污染会导致气候变化，并且还会变得更糟。它对地球有害，因为它会使温暖的天气变暖并产生紫外线。

Why we need to resolve it

Air pollution is harmful to us in multiple different ways. There are 2 main types of pollutants in air: smog and soot. Smog is created when emissions from combusting fossil fuels react with sunlight. Soot are tiny particles of dirt, dust and other types of matter that float around in the air. These things can get into our body through inhaling and can cause damage in our bodies. It will make us more susceptible to pathogens. The emissions from fossil fuels also plays a key part in global warming, which in turn, causes fairly combustible objects to be more dry and more easily combustible, making even more emissions. Thus why we must resolve it.

为什么我们必需解决空气污染？

空气污染以多种不同方式对我们有害。 空气中的污染物主要有两种：烟雾和烟灰。 燃烧化石燃料产生的排放物与阳光反应时会产生烟雾。 烟灰是漂浮在空气中的细小颗粒的尘土，灰尘和其他类型的物质，这些物质可能通过吸入进入我们的体内并可能对我们的身体造成伤害。 这将使我们更容易感染病原体。 化石燃料的排放在全球变暖中也起着关键作用，这反过来又导致相当可燃的物体变得更干燥，更容易燃烧，从而产生了更多的排放量。 因此，我们必须解决它。

Solutions

- People should minimize greenhouse gas and start monitor the amounts of bad gas exhales each day as the lower amount of carbon dioxide and methane and other bad air particles are released, the better

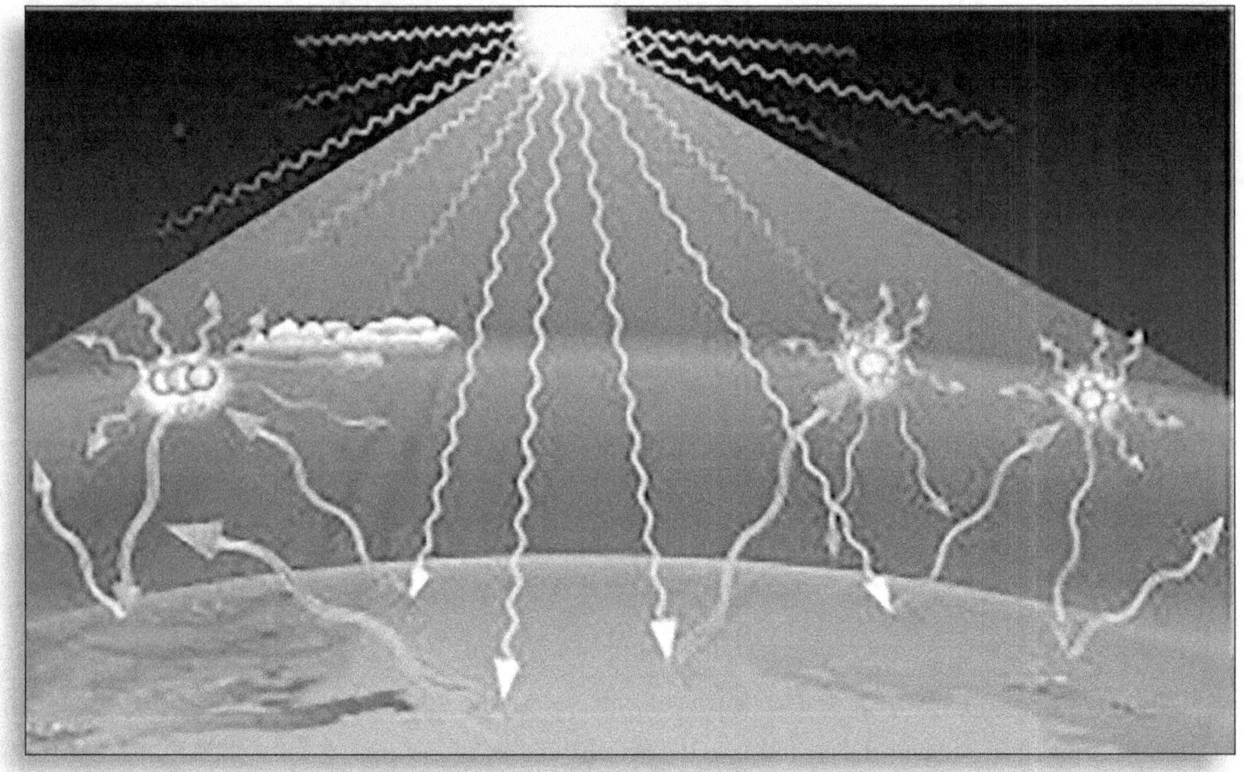

- Use environmental friendly kits for everything such as friendly cleaning kits as much as possible
- Minimize the amounts of car gas polluted into the air as possible

解决方案

- 人们应尽量减少温室气体排放，并开始监测每天排放的有害气体的量。释放出的二氧化碳、甲烷和其他不良空气颗粒的数量應越少越好
- 尽量使用對環境友善的环保器具
- 尽可能减少會造成空气污染的汽车气体量

https://solarimpulse.com/efficient-solutions/opulent-electric-vehicles https://www3.epa.gov/region1/airquality/reducepollution.html

- Stop burning so much fossil fuels.
- Green buildings. A green building can be any sort of structure or building that is made to be eco-friendly. When building these, the design and construction are meant to protect the environment. Waste reduction and efficient use of resources is considered to reduce negative impacts.

- 停止燃烧那么多化石燃料。化石燃料向大气中释放大量二氧化碳，这助长了全球变暖和气候变化。它还会向我们呼吸的空气中释放烟灰，汞和其他有害物质。
- 绿色建筑。绿色建筑可以是生态友好型的任何结构或建筑物。在建造这些房屋时，其设计和建造旨在保护环境。减少废物和有效利用资源被认为减少了负面影响。
- Using more eco friendly energy source alternatives such as electricity, algae, or wind energy and replace them with some of the alternatives
- Don't smoke, or leave flammable objects near fires or combustible objects

- Generally don't make any fire hazards
- 使用更多的生态友好型能源替代品，例如电，藻类或风能
- 减少化石燃料的使用，并用上述某些替代方法替代它们
- 请勿吸烟，或将易燃物品置于火源或可燃物附近
- 不要造成任何火灾隐患

Helen Wang, Mia Han, 卢铭, 吕永泰

Why does smoking become a big issue?

Smoking becomes the main reason for death in the whole world. It causes secondhand smoke. Excessive smoking can damage every organ into your body. It also increases the chances of heart disease. Most of the people didn't realize how serious it is, it causes a lot worse than we can imagine.

Smokers

Nowadays there are 3.2 billion in China, it's almost the total number of developing countries, it also becomes one third percentile in the whole world.

According to WHO, the data has shown the reason mainly cause in death is smoking has over 600 million people, 1 million in China every year, which means in an average every 6 seconds there's one death caused by smoking. Secondhand smoke exposure to nonsmokers has reached overly 600 thousand people.

At this moment one third of over 30 years old male have died because of cigarettes. Lung cancer in China has increased rapidly compared to the rest of the world. 2050, Until 2050, annual death has increased over 3 million. In our country, there are 3 billion smokers, middle school students around 10-15 years old have reached 28.1%, adult male have reached up to 52.9%. As a result, smoking is the main reason that causes lung cancer in 30% and cancer disease 80% in America.

the benefit of reducing smoking

People who smoke have a higher chance to get cancer compared to non-smokers. It's very simple as you can see, the biggest advantages of cancer cells are: it won't spread all over dramatically. If people smoke for a long period of time, the immune system has dropped, then it causes all different types of health issues, cancer cells could easily reproduce. So, smokers should reduce smoking cigarettes or none.

Smoking has dramatically damaged our lungs. And lungs are mainly clean out and refresh our body. If the lung gets damaged, it causes a lot of health issues. Later on, our life has shortened. So reducing smoking has a big impact on our life.

As you can see from the picture on the left, there's a big difference on the lung between smokers and non-smokers.Smoking can cause lung disease by damaging your airways and the small air sacs (alveoli) found in your lungs. Lung diseases caused by smoking include COPD, which includes emphysema and chronic bronchitis. Cigarette smoking causes most cases of lung cancer. Cigar smoking can increase the risk of COPD, and lead to cancers of the lung, oral cavity, and larynx, among other cancers.

Cigarette smoke raises levels of LDL, or "bad"cholesterol, and a blood fat called triglycerides. Those cause waxy plaque to build up in your arteries. At the same time, it lowers HDL, or "good"cholesterol — the kind that prevents plaque from forming.

As for today, in our country there are 10-15% between the age of 9-12 years old; and at least 35% between the age of 12- 15 years old, and at least 75% of teenagers who are over 16 years old and college students.

吸烟对 体的伤害 The damage to your body from smoking 从烟雾中分离出的有害成分达3000余种， 其中主要有尼古丁、烟焦油、 氧化碳等 系 有毒物质。There are at least 3000 chemicals contained in smoking, including nicotine, Tobacco tar, carbon monoxide etc.

Main damage

Nicotine is the main addition to smokers. When you breath in at a certain level it causes cancer, carbon monoxide has toxic damage to your whole body system, especially to your brain. Tobacco contains some chemicals: like tobacco tar and carbon monoxide.

A person who smokes from 15 to 20 cigarettes, has more chances to have lung cancer, oral cancer or throat cancer. Compared to non-smokers, there;s 14 times more.

the damage cause by secondhand smoke

What's secondhand smoke

Secondhand smoke is smoke from burning tobacco products, such as cigarettes, cigars, or pipes. Secondhand smoke also is smoke that has been exhaled, or breathed out, by the person smoking.

- Secondhand smoke contains hundreds of chemicals known to be toxic or carcinogenic, including formaldehyde, benzene, vinyl chloride, arsenic ammonia and hydrogen cyanide.
- Research has shown, Secondhand smoke (SHS) has the same harmful chemicals that smokers inhale. It also causes some serious health problems: like heart attack, cancer, they all contain over 4 thousand chemicals, including at least 50 that can cause cancer.
- For long term effectiveness, there's a lot more chances than smokers.

Solution:

By searching on the internet, we found out some useful tips to stop smoking:

1. Promoting the risk of smoking. As we all know, smoking is bad for us, we should constantly remind people about the disadvantages of smoking.
2. Be clear about the benefit of stop smoking, you can make a plan, and cut down the cigarette daily
3. Distract your attention, whenever we want to smoke, we can distract our attention by keeping us busy, we can do some outdoor activities, whenever we want to smoke, go out and enjoy some meals that you're craving for, it should reduce the desire to smoke.
4. Talk to your doctor or counselor about how to stop smoking, even some meditation or tips.
5. Release yourself. Giving yourself a break is a great way to stop smoking, because it would decrease your pressure, so do be eager to smoke.
6. Avoid drinking or any other possibilities that would cause you to want to smoke.
7. Toss anything that would cause you to smoke. Without those things, it shouldn't cause anyone to smoke.
8. Be active. Whenever you feel like you need a cigarette, try to do some workout. It certainly distracts your attention from smoking.
9. When you reach a goal, reward yourself. For example, if you successfully stop smoking for a week, reward once a week. It should inspire you to stop smoking as early as possible.

Our team has come up with our own idea: Creating a museum for you to stop smoking

In this museum, there's an area for you to use VR glasses to see the whole process of smokers start from non-smoking to healless. At the same time, we prepare some snacks that look like cigarettes, whenever you feel like smoking, just grab these little snacks to distract your attention from smoking.

Cindy Wang

Cindy Wang is a sophomore at Palo Alto High School. In her free time she enjoys solving creative math puzzles, riding thrilling roller coasters and playing soccer. Cindy enjoys volunteering and leads a computer donation project for her club called Interact Club of Silicon Valley. She is interested in astronomy and astrophysics and is currently conducting a research project on it.

Electronic Waste

Hi everyone, my name is Cindy Wang. I'll talk about the harmful effects of electronic waste on our environment. First of all, when you hear the words electronic waste, you aren't really familiar with it or worried by this word compared to words such as global warming or greenhouse gas emissions. However, it's quite ironic because although this is not a common issue talked about, electronic waste has a huge contribution towards greenhouse gas emissions. Electronic waste is a major problem. For example, over 1 billion computers are discarded by this year 2020 and as the access to technology around the world increases, the amount of electronic waste also increases.

The differences between recycling your electronic waste versus just throwing it in the trash is actually huge. Every year in the United States alone, over 30 million computers are thrown away and daily more than 80,000 computers are thrown away instead of being recycled. Daily, if we recycle all our computers instead of throwing it away, we would be able to generate electricity for over 105,000 houses for that day. Thus, instead of throwing away our electricity, if we recycled it, we would be able to generate and save electricity which would also be benefiting our environment.

So what are the benefits of reusing or recycling your computers? Well first, recycling electronics conserves valuable resources and highly engineered materials such as metals, plastics, and gas. It also avoids air pollution and water pollution as well as greenhouse gas emissions. You may wonder, how does it avoid pollution? Well, when people wrongly discard electronics, these electronics are thrown away in landfills and the harmful chemicals in these electronics seep into the Earth or into the ocean. These chemicals can kill marine life in the ocean. Additionally, the chemicals will go into the air when they decompose which will cause air pollution. On the other hand, if we recycle our electronics, we would be able to save energy which will be greatly benefiting our environment.

So what are the dangers of computer waste or discarding it incorrectly? Well, e-waste can harm not only the environment, but also humans. It can cause many diseases such as skin cancer, brain damage, lung cancer, and kidney disease from the harmful chemicals which are polluting the air. As I said earlier, harmful chemicals can also damage our atmosphere and toxic chemicals can seep into the land and oceans, damaging animals and us humans.

Well, what is the solution? If your computer is still in usable condition, you should donate your computers. For example, you can donate your computer to low-income schools or after-school clubs that do not have as much access to electronics. One specific example is that I am part of this interact club which donates computers to kids. This is not only helping the environment, but it also allows kids to have access to electronics whereas they normally would not. On the other hand, if your computer's not in usable condition you can always recycle your computers. In every city, there are always computer recycling drop-offs. You can drop off your computer there and where they can help you correctly recycle your computers.

There are many shocking statistics on e-waste. First, e-waste represents only 2% of Americans' trash in landfills but it equals over 70% of overall toxic waste. This exhibits the significance of this issue. Furthermore, American dump electronics contain over 60 million dollars in gold or silver every year. If we recycle these Electronics, we can conserve these expensive materials. So far, only 12.5% of the electronics in the United States are currently recycled. Increasing this percentage will allow us to greatly benefit our environment.

Thank you very much.